HUGO

SAVAGE KINGS MC - SOUTH CAROLINA

LANE HART

D.B. WEST

COPYRIGHT

SYNOPSIS

Everly Fulton is desperate for a man to come along and sweep her off her feet, giving her a brief reprieve from her hectic life. She's been anxiously awaiting prince charming or a knight in shining armor for years.

What she got instead was a grumpy Savage King who is just passing through town.

Hugo Reddick set out in search of an old hookup. Instead, he finds the woman's bubbly sister raising what may or may not be his daughter.

While trying to figure out how to navigate this potential bombshell, Hugo plans to stay as far away from Everly as possible.

But the more he turns the perky woman down, the harder she pursues him, until he can't resist her for even a second longer.

Neither Hugo nor Everly planned on such a complicated future. And with those complications come obstacles they'll both have to struggle to overcome.

CHAPTER ONE

Hugo Reddick

I have a guilty pleasure.

One that I've never told another soul about.

It's too embarrassing to even admit to my best friend Abel.

He's keeping secrets of his own from me, so I guess we're even. Still, when I hear his boots stomping down our shared hallway, I lunge for the television remote and change the channel before he catches me.

I don't even need to glance over to know Abel will be wearing the same thing as always – jeans, tee, boots, and most importantly, his Savage Kings MC cut, with his black hair shaved close to his head.

Since I haven't gotten a shower yet, I'm lounging in a pair of red athletic shorts I sleep in, pretending to be deep into a car show when Abel leans against the back of the blue recliner that matches my sofa and says, "Want to go to the safe house and fuck Nadia before the ceremony?"

I stretch my arms over my head as I try and figure out how to respond to his question.

Do I like fucking Nadia?

Hell yes.

Is it too early in the day for sex?

Never.

But the thing is, if I don't stop enabling Abel's secret with threesomes where the two of us share a woman, well, he'll never own up to his shit. That's why I respond with one word. "Nah."

"Nah?" Abel echoes, the disbelief heavy in his tone, which means I'm going to have to suck it up and explain myself.

"It's not that I wouldn't mind a quick fuck. It's just...I think I'm over threesomes."

There. It's only a tiny white lie.

"You're what?" Abel shouts, sounding furious.

I shrug one shoulder and keep my eyes on the television so that I don't have to see the hurt on his face when I tell him another small lie. "I've never really liked sharing."

"Then why did you?" he grits out angrily.

"Because I knew you liked it."

"Yeah, what's not to like about both of us being balls-deep in a woman at the same time?"

Ain't that the truth. But I have to put my foot down. Or in this instance, put my dick away so that Abel will maybe, finally, just tell me the truth. He likes pussy and cock. And there's nothing wrong with that.

"It was fun for a while, it's just not really my thing anymore," I reply.

Abel scoffs. "After what, six years it's suddenly not your thing?"

"Bringing home one beautiful woman was just easier than two."

"So, you did it all those years for *convenience*? That's fucking ridiculous, and you know it! You could walk in any bar and have anyone you wanted."

"True enough," I answer, unable to bite back a cocky grin behind

2

my black beard. "Which is why I'm gonna do my own thing from now on and you can do yours. I'm sure you can find another guy to double team with you if that's still what you want to do."

"Where would I find another man willing to do that?" Abel asks. "All the Kings are getting married and shit except for Leo, Marcus, and the prospects. Three of them are hurt, and the other would take a bullet before being near another man's dick."

I bark out a laugh at the mere thought of Marcus, the most possessive, controlling man I know sharing a woman with another guy. "No kidding. The only threesome Marcus would have is with two women. Why don't you give those a try for a while?" I glance over and ask Abel to see his reaction.

Yeah, he doesn't like that idea one bit. "What?" he huffs as if the idea of being with two women is as foreign as riding a crotch-rocket to a Harley rally.

"You and two chicks. It wouldn't be hard to pull off."

"I...yeah, sure, maybe," he mumbles in a rush. "Is that what you're going to do? Fuck two women at the same time?"

"Nah," I answer easily. "I'm done with threesomes, period." I'm getting too old for the fast and loose lifestyle even though I can admit it was fun for a while. "What's the big deal, anyway?" I ask my best friend, trying to give him another nudge to tell me the truth. "Nolan never liked sharing either, and you never gave him hell for it."

"Wait. Are you saying you *never* liked them?" He sounds...hurt, which is not what I intended before he explodes. "You are so full of shit!"

"I didn't mean it that way," I assure him. "Yeah, it was fun, and I enjoyed myself when we were younger and all. Now, I guess I'm just over it."

It's not good for people to lie to themselves. Abel's nearly thirty years old. He needs to own up to his sexuality once and for all.

"Well, fuck you! I'm over this whole goddamn conversation," Abel exclaims before he stomps out of the house, slamming the front door on the way out.

Great. Now he's pissed at me when all I'm trying to do is get him to admit his shit.

That's the reason I've kept my mouth shut for this long – I knew things would change between us, and I fucking hate change more than anything.

Growing up moving from one city or even country to the next, nothing in my childhood was ever the same for more than a few months. I would finally make a friend or two, and then, boom, my dad and I were back on the road, moving into a new house, going to a new school, having to meet new people.

By the time I got to high school, I gave up trying to form any meaningful relationships. There was no reason to get to know a girl before fucking her if I would be leaving in a few months. So, I never bothered.

When it came to friends, well, Nolan and Abel are the only friendships that have lasted more than a year. The sole reason I caved with them was because the three of us were all nomads who were forced to work together. Since patching into the Savage Kings is a lifelong commitment, it was a safe bet that they were going to stick around and that I would too. That's why, when Nolan had to put down roots for the probation office when he was released from prison, Abel and I agreed to get a place with him.

But that didn't last long either.

Just a few years later and here I am, having just moved into a different house across town with Abel because Nolan's getting married tonight.

That's it, though. I'm fucking done moving. I want to live and die within these four walls in this city so that I never have to pack up and move yet again.

Do I expect Abel to live here with me forever? No, it's why the house is in my name only. I've never bought property before, only rented apartments or houses because I knew I was only living there temporarily. Fuck, I really want this place to be permanent.

Nothing ever stays the same, I get that. Shit with Abel is eventually going to change when he decides to be honest with me or he's going to go nuts. One or the other. I just hate that what he decides to do is out of my control.

Going back to the one thing that is within my power at the moment, I press the button on the television remote to flip the channel back to my guilty pleasure again - *Meloney*.

Yeah, it's a crazy as fuck show with lie detector tests about cheating and shocking paternity results, but I'm addicted to the baby daddy drama. I guess it's nice to see that there are plenty of other families just as broken and dysfunctional as mine was growing up.

At least I knew who my father was...

Speaking of which, I hit the volume to turn the sound up when the face of a pretty hippie woman with long, wavy blonde hair appears in the box on the screen. She's not in the studio but videoing in from home.

"Hello, Everly," the host, Marven Meloney says in greeting. "Tell us a little more about why you're on the show today."

"Thank you for having me, Mr. Meloney." She smiles shyly, revealing a slight gap between her two front teeth like she's embarrassed by it, but the imperfection doesn't distract from her beauty at all. "I'm here today for my niece. She's four and such a sweetheart. I've been raising her since she was born, ever since my sister gave birth to her actually. And the thing is, well, my sister was, *is*, rather promiscuous."

"You said that your sister is a stripper, correct?" Meloney asks.

"That's right," blondie answers. "And, you see, when my niece was born, we had a few men take paternity tests, but they all failed, so we gave up. But now, well, she's in Pre-K. The whole school is having a father/daughter dance next month, and it would just mean the world to this little girl if we could find her father."

Holy shit, that's sad as fuck.

The woman's light-colored eyes gloss over, but she's tough and doesn't let a tear fall.

"So, you're here today, asking our audience at home if someone might know or be the father of this little girl? Is that correct?"

"Yes, sir."

"And your sister can't even narrow down who the father *might* be?"

"That's right. All we know is that it's been a little over five years since she was with the man who got her pregnant. At that time, she was living in Cape Cartwright, dancing in a strip club there. Then she moved back home..."

"Oh shit," I mutter aloud as soon as I hear the name of the familiar town. I've spent some time there, and I know they only have one strip club.

"You don't have to give us information about where you live," Meloney assures the woman even though I'm sliding my ass to the edge of the sofa, wanting to know. "You provided us with a photo of your sister. Let's show that to the audience now."

A picture of a tall, raven-haired beauty is plastered on the screen. She's wearing a skimpy silver dress and looks so familiar I have to fight the urge to throw up.

"And this is your sister, Felicity?" Meloney asks the blonde, but it sounds like he's whispering thanks to the sudden roaring in my ears.

"Yes, that's her," she answers.

"Do you have a picture of her daughter, your niece that you would like to share?"

"No, that's...I would rather not have her name or sweet face plastered all over the internet, if that's okay?"

"I understand," Meloney replies. The camera moves away from the blonde to zoom in on his wrinkled face. "If you're just tuning in, we've been talking with Everly, who is asking that any men who had sex with her sister Felicity five years ago in Cape Cartwright to call the number below and schedule a paternity test with the studio. Everly, if we get any leads, we'll be in touch."

"Thank you so much, Mr. Meloney," the blonde says before the show goes to a commercial break.

I sit on the sofa, frozen with fear as I do the math and realize that Abel or I could be the father to some little girl we've never met.

But no, that's ridiculous.

Felicity was no saint. Like her sister said, they've already tested lots of guys. Anyone could be the father.

Anyone.

Abel and I only stayed in Cape Cartwright and fucked the stripper a few times. Well, I guess it was almost every night for a few weeks, up until Nolan got arrested...

Those memories are so old that it takes a few minutes to even remember any of the details. Abel is probably in the clear since he usually called dibs on her ass.

Which means, it's more likely that I...

No. Hell no. I used a condom every single time. The expensive kind of rubbers. The ones that never break.

Abel did too, didn't he?

I mean, he loved knocking on that back door especially when Felicity was giving me head. He wouldn't have forgotten to wrap up, would he? Even though he couldn't get her pregnant with that type of sex, he could still catch whatever the hell STDs the stripper might have been carrying.

I think Abel was careful, but I'm not his father. I don't check his dick to see if he's covered before he slides home. He, however, could probably tell you all about my cock...

Getting up on shaking legs, I go grab my phone from the bedroom, then hold the device in my palm while trying to decide if I should call and tell Abel about Felicity's kid or not.

But dammit, he's already pissed at me. Besides, there's no reason to worry him until I know if there's an actual chance here.

Instead of calling him, I take the phone back to the living room and wait for the number for *Meloney* to flash across the screen again, calling the studio instead.

"Thank you for calling the *Meloney* show. How may I assist you?" a feminine voice asks.

"Ah, yeah, I was wondering if I could get the number for the blonde woman who called in earlier, Everly I think it was. She called for her niece?"

"I'm sorry, sir, but we can't give out anyone's phone number."

"What if I think I might be the father to that little girl?" I ask.

"Then we'll schedule a date and time for you to take the paternity test. We would have to see about scheduling for you to appear on the show with any other..."

"No!" I interrupt. "I don't want to be on the show. I just want to...I want to know more about when Felicity got pregnant."

"Again, I'm sorry, but I can't give you any other personal details."

I hang up on the woman because I don't want to turn this into some circus show for ratings or have anyone knowing my business.

I need to talk to Felicity. But I don't even know where the hell she lives nowadays.

Fuck!

Right now is not the time to panic, though. In just a few hours, I have to be at Nolan's wedding.

Which suddenly reminds me – his bride Rita worked at the same strip club with Felicity. Maybe she knows more about where Felicity went after she got pregnant.

THE WEDDING WAS OVER FAST, thankfully, since it's nearly impossible for me to sit still.

Crazy enough, Abel even caught Rita's garter. I could see the panic on his face when he realized what it meant – that he would be getting married next.

Doubtful as hell, but it's still pretty hilarious to watch him freak out about the age-old tradition.

After the bride and groom take a shit ton of pictures, I try and figure out a way to work Felicity into the conversation with Rita while I have a chance, before she moves on to talk to other guests.

Tomorrow her and Nolan will be leaving for their honeymoon, so it's now or never.

"Rita, whatever happened to that stripper?" I blurt out as we all stand around talking to the happy couple.

The beautiful, strawberry blonde bride smiles at me and says, "You'll have to be more specific since a lot of strippers came and went during the years I worked at the club."

"Oh, right," I mumble. Reaching up, I rub the back of my neck that's burning. "Ah, I mean back when we first started coming with Nolan. Long, raven-haired beauty? I think her stage name was...Felicity."

Abel's suspicious green eyes go as big as saucers, and I know exactly what he's thinking – how do I remember the name of a stripper we fucked five years ago?

"Why do you give a shit about her?" my best friend snaps at me once he recovers from his shock. His voice is so loud that he draws everyone's attention to us. Stammering, he adds, "I mean, that was a long damn time ago."

"She was hot," I answer quickly since it's a better response than the truth.

"Ugh, Felicity," Rita grumbles, obviously not a fan of the woman. "She was a bitch. And Felicity really was her name. I think she up and left a few weeks after you all met her."

"Oh. That's too bad," I reply. "Do you know where she went?"

"No, sorry, I don't," Rita responds with a shake of her head.

"If anyone could find her, it would be Reece," Nolan says as he hooks an arm around his bride and pulls her closer to his side to kiss the top of her head. "He's over there." He points a finger in the direction of where a few Savage Kings from various chapters from all over are gathered. Only one member of the original Savage Kings is in attendance. The uptight man came for the wedding and to spend a week alone with his woman in one of our club's beach houses.

And if I remember correctly, he's an IT genius who can find anything and anyone online.

"Nice!" I say in relief as I start heading in his direction.

"You don't even know her last name!" Abel shouts at my back as I walk away. My only response is a shrug. Guess we'll see if Reece is as good as they say he is.

"Yo, Reece. Sorry to bother you, but I have a sort of, ah, urgent request."

"What do you need?" the former military man asks. He reminds me of my father with his closely cropped buzz cut and no-nonsense attitude.

"I need your help finding someone. A woman."

"One in particular, I'm assuming?" he asks while pulling out his cell phone from his pocket.

"Yes, but I don't even know her last name..."

"I'm not a cop, man. I'm not going to take a sketch or get a statement for the record." Reece sighs. "Look, just tell me what you do know, and I'll find her."

He sounds confident enough, so I give him her name and the location of the strip club where we met Felicity. It doesn't sound like much info to go on, but by some miracle, a few short moments later Reece says, "Found her."

"No shit?" I say in surprise.

"Felicity Fulton."

His fingers move over the keys, then he lifts his face from the screen, arching an eyebrow. "Does your sudden interest in this woman have anything to do with the *Meloney* show earlier today?"

"Damn, you're good," I whisper. The show must have popped up in the search somehow even though I thought they only used her first name. I'm not really sure how, as I don't recognize the software he used to find her. "But, ah, could you not blab about this to anyone? There's no reason to stir shit up on Nolan and Rita's wedding day, you know?"

"I know," Reece agrees. "What's your phone number? I'll text the details to you. It looks like she moved in with her sister in Rockland,

Virginia a few years ago. That's the last address the DMV has for her."

"Thanks, man," I tell him before rattling off my cell number.

Now I just have to figure out how to tell Abel I'm going up north without him trying to come along.

I think it'll do him good if we spend some time apart. It's the reason why I told him I was done with threesomes.

CHAPTER TWO

Everly Fulton

"I saw the show yesterday," Taylor says as we sip our iced teas while sitting in the wicker chairs on my screened-in back porch. Her two little boys are running around the yard while Harley pretends to chase them down in her pink battery-powered Lamborghini. At least I hope she's pretending... Thankfully, Taylor's husband Kyle finishes filling up a water gun from the outside faucet and avoiding him is suddenly the new game.

"Right, the *Meloney* show. Did I look like a complete fool?" I ask her with a wince.

"No, you looked sweet and sad and sort of desperate. Any calls yet?"

"No," I answer with a sigh. "As far as I know, not a single man has asked for a test."

"So, your sister isn't as big of a hoe as we thought she was,"

Taylor remarks, causing me to frown at her. "What? The kids can't hear me and I'm not judging!"

"You were judging a little," I remark. "Most of us aren't lucky enough to fall in love and marry the first boy we dated in high school."

"Oh, Ev. Why do you do that?" Taylor asks.

"Do what?"

"Defend her! Everly, your sister popped out a baby, dropped her in your lap, and peaced out before the umbilical cord was cut."

"Felicity didn't want to be a mother. She knew I did. It made sense for her to leave Harley with me."

"Yeah, you wanted your *own* children after you met Mr. Perfect and got married."

"Sure, doing this all alone for four years has sucked. But I wouldn't change a thing," I say with a smile as I watch Harley throw her arms up and squeal dramatically after a few drops of water lands on the back of her butterfly t-shirt.

When Taylor doesn't say anything else, I glance back over at her. "What?" I ask, noticing her gaze is still focused on me and not the kids.

"You need a man, honey."

I bark out a laugh. "Do I wish I had a partner, a dependable teammate who was in this with me? Yes, absolutely. But I have you, so I'm fine!"

Taylor, of course, refuses to drop the subject. Brushing her long, auburn hair over her shoulder, she asks, "When was the last time you went on a date?"

I take a slow sip of my tea. "I don't really remember," I admit honestly. Lowering my voice, I add, "So long that I've forgotten what it feels like to have a man's hands on me?"

"Was it that creep Rusty Roosevelt four years ago?"

"Ah, probably," I agree with a shrug as if I don't unfortunately recall the last and only time I was naked with that man. I never told Taylor or anyone else the details of that night, and I probably never will. All she knows is that he slept with my very pregnant sister behind my back.

"Rusty the three-pump wonder boy cheater? Oh, Everly. That's just sad!"

Oh right. I told her it was over so fast it barely counted. If only that were true, then maybe I wouldn't have been so traumatized that I can't even get myself off anymore. Rusty never hurt me physically. He just did a number on me psychologically. And he's also my landlord, which makes things super awkward every month whenever I have to see him to pay rent.

"Can you blame me for abstaining for so long after that kind of disappointment?" I respond. "It seemed like so much work, going on date after date, trying to be sexy and sweet and funny before finally ending up in his bed...only for it to be so bad that I wished I had been in my own bed sleeping instead."

Taylor nearly spews her tea at that statement. When she recovers, she says, "The problem with Rusty was that he was too nice, too boring. He probably couldn't blow your mind in bed even if your clit glowed in the dark."

"Taylor!" I exclaim since the kids are just a few feet away.

"They can't hear me over the sounds of their own screams," she says with a dismissive wave of her hand. "And you know I'm right. You need a real man, one who can skillfully navigate his way around a woman's body. One who can make you do some screaming of your own."

It's true that Rusty didn't care about how the sex was for me. No, it was all about his freaky fetish the entire time. How a guy as pretty as him who acted all shy in public could be so messed up in the head in private still boggles my mind.

"Did you hear me, Ev?" Taylor asks. "You need to find yourself an experienced man who can rock your world."

"Oh, you mean one who will jump up and leave before the clock strikes midnight, never to be seen or heard from again? Yeah, I've heard of those kinds of guys who are supposedly so great in bed. I don't believe they actually exist. It's all a bunch of hype."

"There are men who are actually decent human beings and also good at s-e-x. They're just not easy to find," Taylor says with a knowing smile as she eyes her husband, who has a rapidly receding hairline and dad bod but treats her like a queen. "If you don't date for yourself, then you should at least give it another try for Harley, right? So, what if you can't find her biological father? You could still give her and yourself a daddy."

I let the ridiculous daddy kink slide without comment.

"Do you think I haven't tried to find a date? There are no single men in this small town who I'm not related to or who haven't already slept with my sister. Sadly, I think there may even be a few that fall into both categories. Besides, even if I *did* meet someone whom I haven't known my whole life or am not related to by blood, it'll be impossible to leave the house for a night out when I'm everyone's babysitter."

"You could tell people no every once in a while," Taylor remarks.

"Honestly, I'm not sure if anyone even asks me lately. It's just sort of a given that I won't have plans on the weekends."

When you're a single woman approaching thirty in our quaint little community, you may as well start collecting cats because there are no husband prospects.

"You shouldn't feel obligated to watch anyone's brats so they can have weekly date nights when your vagina is all dried up like a prune," Taylor remarks.

I roll my eyes and start to say it hasn't really been that long, but jeez, it really has been years.

Years!

"I'll watch Harley one night a week so that you can give dating a shot," Taylor declares. "Hell, when Kyle is on second shift, you can bring her over every night."

"I can't go out every night! Not when Harley has a bedtime ritual that we have to do every single night, or she gets upset. Then there are lessons to work on, grocery lists to write, meals to plan..."

"Everly, honey?"

"Yeah?"

"Take a deep breath and allow yourself to have a night off once in a while. What time does Harley get tucked in?"

"Seven-thirty, after we read two books, twice each."

"Then make dinner plans for eight."

"You're missing the point here, Taylor. It's hard to make plans when nobody asks me out! There are no single men in this town who I would want to go to dinner with anyway."

"How do you know until you put yourself out there?" Taylor asks.

My cheeks warm, so I hold my glass of tea to each of them as I admit to her, "I, ah, signed up for one of those dating apps a few weeks ago."

"Yeah? Good for you!" Taylor says excitedly.

"Two of them actually. So far, I haven't matched with anyone on either."

Seeing the words "no matches" is even more pathetic than getting stood up. Nobody has swiped right for me. Maybe I need to change my profile picture. As if the photo of my bare legs stretched out in front of me on the beach is the problem and it's not that I've just never been the type of girl men find sexy.

"Which apps?" Taylor asks.

"Ah, Coupled Up, and, um, Uno."

"Uno!" Taylor exclaims. Then she leans closer and whispers, "Girl, that's a hookup app!"

My embarrassed face is now on fire. "Yes, I know that. The name basically says as much! Uno means one, as in one night. Duh."

"So then why..." Taylor starts and then closes her mouth. "Oh. Okay. You'll take the relationship or one night of getting your brains effed out. I get it. Nothing wrong with that either."

I wince at her bluntness, but she's not exactly wrong.

"Are you sure?" I ask in concern. "Is it a bad thing if I wouldn't mind just finally having s-e-x?"

One night to replace the night four years ago would be great even if I never heard from the guy again. An actual orgasm provided by a man would be even better, but beggars can't be choosers.

"No, it's not bad," Taylor says. "As long as you understand it's a fling from the beginning and don't catch any feelings."

"I've never had a one-night stand," I admit.

"I haven't either," she replies with a smile.

"I haven't ever had good s-e-x."

"Never?"

"Nope. Once in high school and then one time in college, both were weeks of dating only to find out they were both awful in bed. Then Rusty was, well, yeah. Is that how it's supposed to be?"

"No. Trust me. I've been married to Kyle for eight years, and he stills makes my toes curl."

"Then you're lucky to have a man who is good to you and good at other things," I tell her.

"Don't I know it," she replies with a smile. "But don't worry, Ev. You'll find your Prince Charming one of these days."

"I really hope you're right."

CHAPTER THREE

Hugo

Well, this one-story brick structure is it, the address Reece gave me for Felicity in Rockland, Virginia.

Guess it's now or never.

I came all this way for a reason, not to just sit on my damn bike and stare at the place, which I can't help but notice desperately needs to have the gutters cleaned and a new roof.

Forcing myself to grow a pair, I climb off my Harley, then march up the three steps to the front porch. My finger isn't shaking when I ring the doorbell. Well, not much. I hold my breath as I wait for the door to open, trying to figure out what the fuck to even say now that I'm here.

"Yo, Felicity. Remember fucking me and Abel five years ago? Well, is one of us the asshole who knocked you up?" seems like the best way to go.

Then it occurs to me that the blonde hippie from the *Meloney* show might answer instead of the raven-haired stripper. If so, saying, *"Hi, I think there's a chance that I knocked up your sister"* doesn't seem like a great idea. She'll wonder how I got her address since the show wouldn't give it out. I would either have to lie or admit that I had an IT genius track Felicity down, making me sound like a stalker.

Fuck, would someone just open the goddamn door and put me out of my misery already?

No one does come to the door, unfortunately, no matter how long I stand there sweating bullets.

But eventually, I do hear a few child-like squeals coming from around back.

It's a nice fall night, so they must be outside.

For some reason, I just can't picture Felicity as the kind of mother who runs around the backyard playing with a little kid in her stilettos and skimpy dresses.

Still, some adult must be watching the brat, so I jog down the porch steps and start walking around back where I come to a stop at the six-foot privacy fence with a combination lock on the gate.

The happy squeals are louder from here, but there's also the murmur of two women having a conversation most likely on the screened-in back porch. Neither of them sounds loud and obnoxious like Felicity.

Not that I remember much about her other than she was the life of the party and gave great head.

"There's nothing wrong with you, Everly!"

Well, that's one question answered. It's Felicity's sister and... someone else.

"You've just had bad luck with guys. It's time to get back out there!" the other female exclaims.

"I don't want Harley to get her hopes up, so for now, I think I should maybe just try and keep dating...casually, if you know what I mean."

That has to be Everly talking. And did she say the girl's name is

Harley? As in the brand of my and Abel's cherished motorcycles? That doesn't bode well for us.

"You mean hookups on Uno?" the friend asks.

The hippie is on Uno? No shit. She didn't look like the type of girl to meet up with strange men and bang them without even having a meal with them first.

That's exactly what the app is for – easy, no-hassle fucks. Which is why I even pulled it up as soon as I got myself a motel room in town. There was only one woman within a sixty-mile radius, and you bet your ass I swiped right after seeing her long, beautiful tan legs and imagined them wrapped around my waist.

"I know it's not like me," the woman says. "Felicity was always the pretty, outgoing, sexy one. I've lived in her shadow my entire life, you know? For once, I would like to be wanted too."

Felicity literally loves the spotlight. It's why she decided to get naked and strip in front of strangers. Growing up, I have no doubt that the woman hogged all the attention away from her sister and any other females around.

"Give me your phone!" her friend says.

"What? Why?"

"We're going to find you a man."

"Fine, but it's pointless. There are no hot men within a ten-mile radius."

Why only ten miles? I can't help but wonder.

"Why ten miles?" the other woman thankfully asks for me.

"Because I want to stay in town to meet them, not meet up with a stranger in a strange city alone, you know?"

"Smart," her friend says, and I have to agree with that decision.

"Oooh, you're in luck!" the friend declares. "There's a new guy in town, and he's...wow, he's close. Like really close, less than half a mile away. There, I swiped, and it's a match! Oh, and I just sent a message for you saying, 'Hi handsome.'"

"Taylor!" Everly exclaims just as my fucking phone dings. It

21

sounds like a goddamn gong being hit in the quiet yard, making me wince.

I quickly pull the device from the inner pocket of my leather cut to silence it as one of the women says, "Did you hear that?"

"Hear what? Your box cheering? Nope."

"Haha. Not funny," Everly replies. "Well, at least let me see this guy you think is hot. What if I think he's ugly?"

"Trust me, you won't."

"How can you be so...*oh*," Everly says before going silent.

I hold my breath, because I'm pretty sure she's looking at my damn picture. What does 'oh' mean? Is that a good 'oh' or a bad 'oh'? I've never had any problem getting women in my bed, so I've never really questioned how I looked until now, for some reason.

Jesus, woman, put me out of my misery already! Say something else!

I'm not sure why it matters what the pretty little blonde thinks about me, but it does. My ego needs her approval.

"Well?" her friend eventually prompts for me. "What do you think of him?"

"He's...he looks strong, like the kind of man who could toss me around like a ragdoll."

"You mean throw you down and eff your brains out?"

"Yeah, that too," Everly says, followed by a sigh. Then both women are giggling like schoolgirls.

"After no sex for four years, you're diving right into the deep end."

Four years? The blonde has gone four years without sex? How is that possible?

My dick gets hard at the prospect of taking her up on that challenge before I quickly push those thoughts away. I won't think about her sighing after I make her come for the third time in a row with my tongue or how I bet she is light enough to throw around or position every which way.

As I quietly walk away back to my bike, I try to figure out if I should ignore the message on the app or respond.

A date with the blonde could be the best way to find out where the fuck Felicity is and get closer to her daughter so that I can try and figure out if there's any resemblance to me or Abel.

It seems like a better plan than explaining to a complete stranger how I tracked her ass down.

Yeah, a date is much better.

I'll just have to remember to keep my hands to myself.

That shouldn't be all that hard while there's the constant reminder of a kid that could be mine hanging over my head.

CHAPTER FOUR

Everly

"Are you nervous? You look nervous," Taylor says as I try on the third outfit the next night while she critiques each from her seat on my bed. Apparently, I don't own any "date" clothes.

"Of course I'm nervous! I can't even figure out what to wear. How will I know what to say?"

"Just calm down. It'll all come to you. Either the bearded biker will be hot in person and things will click, or they won't and then you leave and come home," she replies. "But really, girl, if it feels right, go for it."

I stop riffling through the hangers in my closet to turn around and face her. "You mean just hook up with him? How will I know if it feels right?"

"If you feel that special flutter in your panties, that's your body's way of telling you it's right, even if your head isn't sure about being so naughty."

"That's really a thing?" I ask. "The, um, flutter?"

Taylor stares at me, her face blank. "No man has ever made you wet before you got into bed with him?"

"Ha! No man has ever made me wet down there period, even during sex," I admit honestly.

"Oh, you poor thing," she says, her blue eyes full of pity as I turn my back to her to keep searching for a date outfit.

"Are you messing with me right now or not?" I ask since I can't ever tell with her.

"No, Everly. I swear I'm not lying. You've been deprived for way too long. I hope it goes well tonight."

"Me too."

"Just a heads-up, though," Taylor starts. "Some men are a little selfish and impatient. They need to get their good time before they become generous enough to repay the favor."

I turn back around to face her with a frown. "So, *I* have to make the first move? No. No way!"

"If he gives you the tingles in your panties, then you'll be singing an entirely different tune. You'll do anything for some relief from that yearning. Trust me."

"I've never felt any of those kinds of urges. I really think there's something wrong with me."

"Oh, there is definitely something wrong with you, honey," Taylor agrees. "You've been picking the wrong men. Ones who play it way too safe. That obviously doesn't do it for you, so it's good that you're ready to...expand your horizons."

"I'm all for expanding horizons. It's just...I don't want to end up like Felicity, you know?" I admit softly.

"That would be impossible. First, you would have to sleep with every man in town, relatives included." I wince but can't argue that statement of fact. I'm thankful that Harley isn't the result of any of those stupid, disturbing flings from their teenage years. "Then, you would have to sleep with half of the male population of the United States to catch up to Felicity's dick count."

"She's not that bad," I say in my sister's defense. "But she is rather promiscuous."

"One one-night stand won't lead you down the path of whoredom, Ev. If anything, it'll do your body good. Your mind too. A woman needs to feel attractive, desired at least once in a while."

"I haven't felt desired in a very long time." How could I when Felicity always stole the attention by wearing the least amount of clothing possible? Then, the few years she was away, living in Cape Cartwright, I was too busy studying at college to date. Now, when I want her here helping me out, she hardly ever comes around because that would mean seeing and interacting with her daughter.

"Hopefully that will all change tonight!" Taylor says excitedly. "Pick something to wear, then go and have fun. If you don't hurry up, you're going to be late."

"But Harley..." I start with a glance in the direction of her bedroom.

"She's sound asleep. I'll watch the wild child like a hawk," Taylor promises. "Kyle is home with the boys, so I can stay as late as you need me to."

"I'll be back by eleven."

"Uh-huh. Sure thing."

"What? I will!" I assure her.

There's no way that anything with this random guy I've never met before and only said a few words to through an app is going to click. Giving up, I go back to the first outfit I tried on – a white, cable-knit sweater dress since the nights are starting to get chilly along the coast. Then, I just have to decide on what shoes to wear with it...

"Here," Taylor says, reaching down to unzip her tall, brown suede boots. "You need these more than I do," she tells me while struggling to pull one of the boots off.

"What? No. I can't wear your favorite boots to a bar! They could get dirty!"

Laughing as she hands them both to me, Taylor says, "Girl, it would be worth it for you to finally have a chance to feel the tingles. And they would look perfect with that dress."

"Not the brown booties?"

"No, knee-high is definitely the way to go, trust me."

"Okay, if you're sure?" I ask for confirmation as I take the soft suede boots from her.

"I am sure, so go get changed and get your ass out the door!"

"Fine. I'm going!" I reply with a sigh.

Hugo

I've never been on a fucking date before.

It's a statistic I used to be proud of, a badge of honor that I didn't have to wine and dine women to get them naked.

Now, I'm sort of regretting it, feeling like I'm way out of my league.

Fucking a woman is easy. Keeping my hands off of her body and having an actual conversation, how the hell do I do that?

I thought that our 'date' would be cut short when I showed up at the door for Everly and got to talk to Felicity about the kid.

But when I offered to pick up the blonde hippie from her place, Everly refused.

Not that I really blame her.

After all, I'm a strange man she met on a hookup app. Not someone you would want to know where you live before you see them for the first time.

What little I know about the blonde from seeing her on television for a few seconds and overhearing a conversation with her friend, she doesn't look like the type to meet men for a quick fuck. Then again, she said she hasn't been with a man in years.

28

Years!

That's not something I can even comprehend. Sex is like a regular clockwork routine for me. I wake up, work on my bike, handle any club shit, then bring a woman home from a bar or go to her place to fuck her with Abel.

Not that I'll be doing that again with my best friend.

The truth is, I can't remember the last time that I was alone with a woman. The threesomes became a ritual for us, one that worked well enough for me and Abel both to have a good time and get the releases we needed. Nothing screams *"I'm not looking for a commitment"* like sharing a woman with another man. Any woman who agreed to the arrangement obviously couldn't misunderstand that it was only about no-strings attached sex for us, which alleviated any stage five clingers.

Abel's an ass man, so women who are into threesomes are about the only ones who would let him in the back door. And I love watching a woman struggle to take my entire dick down her throat. Hearing those hums of approval and eager little whimpers, feeling the sounds vibrate around my shaft, it's what gets me off faster than anything else. Sucking me off while she's getting fucked causes a non-stop symphony of sexy noises. So, Abel and I both got exactly what we needed at the same time.

Not that we were selfish lovers. We both love eating pussy while fingering all their holes, getting a woman good and ready for the pounding we planned to give her.

Great, and now I'm about to get hard just thinking about that shit as I wait on a stool at the bar of *Gritty Greer's*, the one and only place you can buy a cold beer in this small coastal town.

Aroused is the last thing I want to be since this date is not about getting my dick wet but about...hell, I can't even remember what it's about when the door opens and a beautiful blonde walks through it. She's showing off her long legs in tall, fuck-me boots and a dress that stops just above her knees. There's a teasing hint of skin between the two pieces of clothing just begging for a hand or mouth to climb up and explore between those tan thighs.

When the boots start to come closer, I eventually force my gaze higher, lingering over the swell of hips and nice round tits a few extra seconds before I finally get to her face.

Oh shit.

"Hi! Are you Hugo?" Everly Fulton, Felicity's sister, asks me with the same shy smile from the television screen. That little gap between her front teeth is even more adorable in person.

"Ah, yeah. I'm Hugo." That's when I'm suddenly reminded of the nickname *Huge-Ohhh* the stripper gave me years ago thanks to the tightness in my jeans at the moment.

I can't move. Can't stand up. Can't fucking think at the moment. I'm like a teenager seeing a naked woman for the very first time. Except this is worse. I'm a grown ass man and I've not only seen but had dozens of naked chicks underneath me. The woman before me is still fully dressed.

"Nice to meet you. I'm Everly," she says as she hops right up on the empty stool next to mine, causing the hem of her dress to creep up her smooth, tan thighs a few more teasing inches.

I try to remind myself that this isn't a real date. I'm not going to be sliding my palms up her legs later to see if her skin is as soft as it looks or running my tongue through her folds to find out if she tastes as sweet as she seems.

No, after keeping an eye on the house all day without a glimpse of her, I need to find out where the hell Felicity is so I can ask her if there's an actual chance her kid is mine or Abel's. Failing that, I need to get a look at the brat to see if she has my hazel eyes or Abel's green ones.

The reminder of possibly having a dependent finally has some of my brain cells deciding to work again.

"Can I get you a drink?" I ask, barely refraining from asking if I can pour it down her chest and lick it off the swell of her tits.

Fuck, I need to get a grip. I'm pretty sure a guy isn't supposed to be thinking about the woman naked the entire time they're on a date.

"A water would be fine," Everly responds, which of course has me thinking about her standing under a showerhead, water dripping down her bare, sexy curves. And hell, now I'm thirstier than I think I've ever been before.

"Two waters!" I call out to the bartender.

"Keep your panties on!" the grumpy man behind the bar shouts back. He does a double take at the woman beside me and his scowl eases. "Oh, hey, doll! I'll be right with you," he tells her, completely changing his tone from annoyed to sugary sweet.

"Thanks, Greer," Everly replies, flashing him a warm, closed-lip smile like it was made just for him.

No wonder the bartender is nice to her. How could anyone treat her badly when she looks and acts like a saint?

While we wait for our water in silence, Everly looks at me and then away several times while pushing her long, wavy hair behind her ears, like maybe she's nervous too. I know I need to say something to her to break the ice, I'm just not sure what.

"So, are you new to town?" she asks me before I can think of anything.

"Ah, no. Just passing through."

"Oh. So, are you in the area for business or pleasure?" Her eyes, a light grayish-blue I notice, widen and her cheeks redden when she realizes how that sounded. "I meant, are you here for work or on vacation?"

"Work, yeah. Just driving right on through for work," I lie. "I've been, ah, meeting with chapters up north."

Shit, why am I rambling and making shit up?

"Chapters?"

"MC chapters. Motorcycle clubs?" I point to the small white patch that says "Myrtle Beach" on the right side of my chest.

"Oh. You ride a motorcycle? What kind?"

"A 2020 Fatboy. It's a thirtieth anniversary special edition. Only twenty-five hundred were ever made."

Jesus, there I go again, talking about my damn bike like she gives a shit

"Wow, I bet that's a nice one," Everly remarks.

Thankfully, the bartender finally slides the two glasses of water in front of us just in time to shut me up. I pick up mine and guzzle more than half of it.

Everly only sips at her water, probably trying not to wash off or smear her pretty pink lipstick. It's the only thing pink I've ever wanted to wear. I wouldn't mind if it stained my neck, chest, stomach, or my dick.

Have I mentioned blowjobs are my favorite thing in the world?

And I know all men love them, but really, I would choose mouth over any other body part about ninety percent of the time. Same goes for pussy. I would rather tongue it than a chick's mouth. Maybe because oral feels amazing for everyone, and it can't accidentally knock a woman up.

Which reminds me why I'm here just as I start to drown in her gorgeous, expectant eyes.

"What do you do? You know, for work?"

"Oh, I teach the second grade."

"A teacher? Yeah, I can see that about you," I tell her.

She smiles shyly, hiding the cute, little gap.

"Are you close with your family?" I ask Everly. Which sounds a little random and nuts coming up out of the blue.

When she glances away, I know it was the wrong thing to say.

"Ah, not really, no. My mom is a housewife, and my dad is a professional poker player, which means they usually don't have a dollar to their names. And then there's my sister and a ton of cousins."

"Older or younger sister?" I ask.

"Older by just two years."

"Yeah? You two must be close since you're almost the same age," I remark, trying to get her to talk about Felicity.

"No, we're not. My sister pretty much comes and goes out of my life constantly."

"Oh."

Fuck. Does that mean Felicity no longer lives with Everly?

"What about you?" blondie asks before I can pry any more information out of her about her sister.

"What about me?"

"Are you close with your family?"

"Ah, no."

I try to end it at that, but Everly blinks her long, dark lashes at me expectantly.

"It was just me and my dad growing up. He's a public affairs officer for the Army, so we traveled a lot when I was a kid."

"That sounds like it would be exciting but also...lonely."

"Yeah," I say, since those two emotions pretty much sum up my childhood.

"If you two aren't drinking, then get off my stools so someone else can," the bartender suddenly snaps at us.

"Sorry, Greer," Everly replies as she hops down from the stool beside me immediately. I'm still sitting there glaring daggers at the asshole when I feel a feather-light touch on the back of my clenched fist that's resting on the top of my thigh. I look down and watch as Everly's fingertips trail over my knuckles, then squeeze my fingers. "Want to head outside, get some air?"

"Air? Yeah, sure."

I'm not used to a woman touching me so carefully. Usually I get my bicep, ass, or dick squeezed while being asked her place or mine.

Guess that's why I never hook up with good girls – they don't go around grabbing guys' junk and asking for a hot fuck.

As soon as we walk out of the bar, Everly lifts her hair off the back of her neck, raising that damn dress to show a little more skin between the hem and top of her tall, sexy boots.

"Nice dress," I can't help but blurt out. What's with being around this woman and running my mouth?

"Ah, thanks," she replies as she drops her arms and smooths her hands over her sides, highlighting that perfect, hourglass figure that's a little heavier on the bottom, just the way I like it. "I figured it would be easy to get on and off."

Wait. Back the fuck up.

What did she just say?

Unable to form words, I stammer a simple, "Huh?"

Those innocent eyes blink at me several times before she says. "Oh, I mean, I guess we could do it without taking our clothes off. If that's what you want?"

Holy shit.

She's seriously talking about getting naked with me right now.

I guess I shouldn't be surprised since she was on the Uno app, but still, she seems so sweet and shy. Although, she did tell her friend it's been four years since she's had sex...

Oh, fuck me. The things I could do to that hot little body would blow her mind. I could have her on her back, legs wrapped around my head, dripping wet and begging for more before she knew what hit her. She would come so many times on my tongue that she wouldn't be able to walk for hours.

"Should we go back to your place?" Everly asks, snapping me out of imagining her stumbling around naked like Bambi after so many orgasms.

"My place?" I exclaim in confusion. "You mean my small, shitty motel room? It smells like garbage and has paper-thin walls. The whole place can probably hear me when I sneeze."

"Then I guess you'll just have to put something in my mouth to keep me quiet so they don't hear us, won't you?"

Jesus Christ, yes.

Wait, no.

"I can't. We can't do that," I blurt out.

34

And instantly I want to take the words back when her pretty face falls. God, she looks so disappointed that it physically hurts me.

"I thought that was the whole point..." she starts and then blinks at me. "Oh, you're not...you don't..."

"I *am* attracted to you, Everly. That's not it," I rush to explain since I don't want to hurt her feelings.

"Then why don't you want me?"

Those are the most heartbreaking words I've ever heard because that statement sounds like it's about more than just me rejecting her.

"I do want you, but I'm just passing through town."

"Yeah? So, then what's the problem? We matched up on the Uno app. I'm obviously not expecting anything more than one night."

"I know, I just, I don't want to take advantage of you."

"Hugo?"

"Yeah?"

"Don't make me beg you for this."

Oh fuck.

"That's not...you don't really want to do this."

"Believe me, I really do," she says. "Is it because you think I'm too young? I'm older than I look."

"No, it's not that."

Fuck, I'm running out of excuses, and I can't think straight, not with all of my blood rushing south to where my throbbing dick is hurting so damn bad it might burst if I don't free it from my jeans soon.

"How about if I do you and then you do me?" she asks while coming a step closer to slide her hand down to where I ache to rub me through the denim. I can't manage to speak a word as she pops the top button and starts to lower my zipper down. No, I'm too busy thinking three steps ahead to when she's on her knees and I'm in her mouth.

No, I can't go there with her. Especially not right outside of the fucking bar! Fuck, that would be hot, though...

There's a kid that might be mine, and here I am being selfish and only thinking about getting off.

Grabbing both of Everly's hands, I pull them up and away from my pants. Pressing them to her chest, my knuckles graze her tits and I almost change my mind. Damn, it's harder than I expected to not touch her.

"I need to go. I'm sorry," I say in a rush before I'm unable to walk away. "I do want to see you again. I'll call tomorrow," I assure her, not knowing if that's a lie or not.

My Harley is thankfully close, so I'm on it and peeling out of the parking lot as fast as possible.

Tomorrow, Everly will come to her senses and be glad nothing happened between us. I'll call Reece and ask him to keep looking for Felicity since I'm not getting anywhere here.

I'm not sure if I'm hoping he can't find her so I have to see Everly again, or praying he does so this nightmare can be over.

CHAPTER FIVE

Everly

"Wow, you're home early," Taylor says, sitting up from her seat on the sofa where she was watching the television on a volume too low to actually hear. When I stand there frozen just inside the door, she lowers her feet from the matching ottoman to the floor to stand up. "The date didn't go well?"

"No. Well, I don't think so," I tell her before remembering his promise to call tomorrow even though it seemed like he couldn't get away from me fast enough. "Honestly, I have no idea," I finally admit.

"What do you mean you have no idea? How about you come sit down and start from the beginning."

I nod as I go over and we both take a seat on the sofa.

"Did he catfish you? The actual guy was not the one in the picture?"

"Oh, no. It was definitely the same guy in the photos. If anything, he looks even better in person – gruff and sexy with his ruffled black hair, beard long enough to tug on, and a deep, rumbly voice."

"Okay. That's all good. Did you just not feel the tingles?"

"Oh, I felt them," I admit to her. Boy, did I feel them as soon as I saw the big, muscular man sitting at the bar looking like a naughty dream. "But, um, I guess he didn't."

"Huh?"

"I asked if he wanted to go back to his place, to his motel room, and he turned me down."

"What? No way!" Taylor exclaims. Then, lowering her voice to avoid waking Harley, she asks, "Did he say why not?"

"Something about his motel room was shitty and he didn't want to 'take advantage of me,' but that doesn't make any sense, right? I mean, we matched on a hookup app."

"Exactly. The date was just the necessary step to meet up and get to the naked part."

"You would think, but he said no. Stopped me before I..." I barely refrain from admitting to my best friend that I tried to give him a blowjob in the parking lot of Greer's bar. That makes me sound pathetic, and it's something Felicity would have done. Except no man ever turns her down. "He didn't even kiss me goodnight before he bolted out of there," I inform Taylor.

"Huh," she mutters, looking as confused as I feel.

"I didn't really think he liked me. He said he was attracted to me and even asked to see me again."

"That's a good sign."

"Should I agree? If he even calls. I feel so stupid and confused."

"Maybe he just doesn't want to rush into anything. Or maybe his motel room is shitty, and he was embarrassed."

"Well, I'm not going to invite him here!"

"No, of course not," Taylor agrees. "But there's no reason to turn down another date if you thought he was hot and there were flutters."

"Sure, one more date won't hurt anything except my pride."

"Don't think that way, Ev! You're beautiful and sweet. Any guy would be lucky to date you," my best friend assures me.

"Date me but not sleep with me on the first night. I know it shouldn't bother me. If we had...I probably *would* have regretted it." Sex means trusting another human being enough to be naked and vulnerable with them. The last time I trusted a guy enough to go to bed with him I felt icky afterward, not just for days or weeks but still years later. And that was a man I had been dating and thought I was getting to know, not a complete stranger.

"Then, see! Everything happens for a reason," Taylor remarks.

"Maybe."

"If he asks you out again, tell him you'll go to dinner with him. It's more date-ish than a beer at the bar."

"Neither of us had any alcohol," I tell her.

"Then there's your problem! You need to loosen up. Maybe he does too."

"He could've had a drink before I got there. I'm not sure. But we both had water while we sat and talked at the bar."

"What did you talk about?" she asks.

"The normal things. He asked me a ton of questions about myself and my family. Mostly, he listened, and I just talked his ears off." I think back to our conversation, realizing, "In fact, I barely got any information out of him. His name is Hugo, and he lives at Myrtle Beach. He's in town on some sort of 'club business,' whatever that means."

"Well, it sounds like he could be one of those quiet, hot guys who doesn't say much but is deeper than he looks."

"Maybe. I don't know. He seemed sort of annoyed the whole time. Like he didn't really want to be there with me and couldn't wait until it was over."

"That's just your self-doubt messing with your head. Don't listen to that bitch. You should go out with him again. Tomorrow night."

"I can't..." I start to say, and Taylor holds up her palm to stop me.

"Tomorrow is Friday night. Harley can come sleep over. She'll have fun playing with the boys."

"Harley sleeping is much different from awake Harley," I whisper. "You know she can be a handful. Her teachers say she's...that she's a bully to the other kids."

"That sounds like a bunch of bologna to me," Taylor replies, easing some of my worry. My best friend and her family have spent more time with Harley than anyone besides me. "She's just a tough girl, and the rest of the kids are probably little pussies."

"Taylor!"

"Parents nowadays are way too protective. Kids are going to be kids. Only the strong survive."

"It's Pre-K, not Lord of the Flies!"

"Harley will be fine. So what if she pushes around some kids? They probably deserve it. Did you think about that?"

"When I ask her why she hit someone or knocked them down, all she tells me is that they were big jerks. When I tell her she shouldn't call her classmates jerks, she doesn't say anything else about it."

"She's not a bully to my boys. If she was just being mean to be mean, I think she would've made them bleed by now. But she hasn't, because she's not a bad kid."

"I hope you're right," I say with a sigh.

"I am always right. Just ask my husband," Taylor jokes, making me smile.

"Thank you for staying with her tonight. And if Harley wants to have a sleepover with Carson and Charlie tomorrow night, then I'll tell Hugo yes to another date *if* he actually calls or texts."

"Good," she says before she stands up and stretches her arms over her head. "It was nice getting to sit in a quiet room without anyone asking me for anything for a few hours."

"All moms need a break once in a while," I tell her.

"Yes, *you* do," she replies.

While I may be Harley's main caregiver and guardian, I can't think of myself as her mother. Not when Felicity is her real mom, always coming and going out of her life.

Sometimes I wonder if it would be better for Harley if Felicity didn't come around at all, confusing her even more.

But I can't do that. I won't remove my sister from her daughter's life no matter how much I wish I could.

CHAPTER SIX

Hugo

I wish I had someone to talk to about what's going on with Felicity and Everly. An outsider who can tell me what I should do.

But Nolan is on his honeymoon with his new wife, and I don't want to tell Abel and freak him out unless I have to.

So that leaves me with nothing but pacing around my small motel room that smells like stale cigarettes and trash.

The thought of bringing someone like Everly back here to fuck her is unimaginable. She's the kind of woman who probably likes candles, flower petals, and whatever other feminine bullshit some women like to set the mood.

Felicity, on the other hand, wouldn't bat an eye at the brown and yellow décor from the seventies or think twice about any stains on the mattress.

Not that I'll be hooking up with her here even if I do find her.

What are the odds that she's holed up in that house, refusing to come out?

Slim but not impossible.

Although, I think Everly would've mentioned last night if her sister was squatting in her house.

Damn, I wish I had someone to talk to, a voice of reason to give me advice so I don't fuck this up.

There is one person who sort of has an idea about what's going on, what I'm doing up here.

I decide to call Reece even though I'm pretty sure the military man is trying to have a nice, relaxing vacation with his wife.

"Yeah?" he answers on the first try.

"Sorry to bother you. I'm up here in Virginia at the address you gave me, but there's no sign of Felicity."

"Then I don't know what to tell you. Maybe she changed her name."

"Nah, she wouldn't have done that," I reply.

"I'll do a more thorough search once I get home this weekend."

"Okay, thanks, Reece."

"You on your way back to Myrtle Beach?"

"Ah, no. Not yet. I'm going to stay up here in case she pops up."

"Pops up?" Reece repeats. "What do you mean?"

"Felicity's kid is here with her aunt."

"Oh, you mean the kid that you think might be yours?"

"I don't fucking know that. I need to talk to Felicity."

"Come on, man. You wouldn't have gone to all the trouble of riding up there the day after you found out she had a kid unless you had an inkling."

"An inkling is all it is," I assure him. "Although, I haven't seen her yet, so..."

"You're still there because you want to see the kid, aren't you?"

"Maybe."

"Just be careful. You don't want people to think you're some pervert."

"I know that," I huff. "Have you told anyone?"

"No."

"Good. Don't. Even if they ask."

"Why would they ask me about where you are?" Reece questions.

"Because I'm avoiding Abel. There's a small chance the kid could be his. I don't want him to freak out until I feel things out. And if I talk to him, well, he'll know something is up with me."

"I won't lie for you, but I know how to bend the truth when I need to," the no-nonsense man replies.

"Good. That's all I'm asking. Thank you."

"I'll be in touch, and you better answer my fucking call."

"I will," I assure him with a chuckle.

"And don't get arrested on any stalker charges."

"I won't," I promise and then I end the call to do just that.

But first, I type out a text message to Everly and quickly send it before I chicken out.

Sorry about last night. It really was me, not you. You're great. Can I see you tonight?

After the way things ended, I'm not sure if Everly will even respond to my text that sounds like a teenager wrote it, much less consider meeting me for another 'date.'

I don't have a lot of experience turning women down. That's just not something I've ever had to do in my life.

Women come and go, one right after another. That's the way I prefer it. No attachments. No commitments.

Now I'm supposed to figure out a way to get to know a beautiful woman without falling into bed with her or having her realizing I'm trying to track down her sister to see if I knocked her up.

Yeah, there's no instruction manual for how to navigate these dangerous waters.

Needing to get out of the stifling motel room, I step outside and lock the door, intending to go do a little stalking.

"Hey, man!" a man's voice shouts from behind me.

When I turn around, I see a guy in torn jeans and a ratty tee, his dirty blond hair long enough to fall in his eyes. He straightens from where he was working on an old Panhead Harley near the front office door. "You need to stay another night?" he asks, which is when I realize he must work there. It was a woman who checked me in the night before last.

"Ah, yeah, if that's okay?" I tell him.

"Sure thing. We're not exactly at capacity, as you can tell," he replies with a jerk of his chin toward the lot that's empty other than my bike and two other cars.

"That's a nice Panhead you've got there."

"Thanks. Not as new and pretty as your Fatboy, but she gets me where I need to go. Most of the time."

"Yeah, I hear you."

He grabs a towel and starts wiping his hands on it as he comes toward me. "There's not a Savage Kings chapter within a hundred miles, so you're not really here for the club, are you man?" he asks, catching me by surprise.

Fuck. Was he in the bar last night? I don't remember seeing him. Must have been another guy who overheard and told him about my conversation with Everly. Maybe the bartender?

"Jesus, man. Calm your tits. You don't have to tell me all your deep dark secrets," the asshole says with a chuckle. "As long as you're not here to raise hell in my city, then we're good. Name's Remy, and I own this shithole motel."

He holds out his hand and I shake it, not bothering to challenge him on the assertion that it's *his* city or disagree that his motel is, in fact, shitty.

"I'm Hugo, and I'm not here to raise any hell," I assure him. "In fact, I don't even know what I'm doing here."

"Greer said you met up with one of our local girls at the bar last night," he says, confirming my suspicion about the nosy ass bartender. "If you had brought Everly back to your room last night, you wouldn't be welcome in my motel or town another night."

46

"That right?" I ask with a smirk. I'm not used to anyone standing up to me when I'm wearing my cut. Guess the Kings' reputation hasn't made its way this far north yet.

"That's right. We take care of our own," he says. "Everly's a good girl. Not sure how you got up with her, but if you so much as make her eyes shimmer, we'll kick your ass."

"*We*, huh?" I make a show of looking around the empty lot. "Looks like it's just you and me out here right now, buddy."

"Everly's my cousin, and we have a big family."

"Don't worry. I don't plan to lay a finger on your cousin," I tell him truthfully.

"Then you've got the self-control of a saint."

I lift my eyebrows at that statement, since it's an odd one coming from a blood relative.

"She's gorgeous and you turned her down. Why is that?"

Damn. Was there a camera watching us outside the bar? Good thing I didn't let her pull my cock out.

"That's between me and her," I tell him. "Isn't anything in this town private, or do you all eavesdrop on everyone all the time?"

He shrugs. "It's a small town, not much to do. Gossiping is one of our favorite pastimes."

"Gossip and Harleys, huh?"

"That's about it, unless there's a football game on TV."

I shake my head and smile. "Trust me, I plan to leave as soon as I can."

"As soon as you can? Ain't nobody making you stay here," he remarks at the same time my phone dings with a new message.

I pull out the device from inside my cut pocket and see a new message from Everly.

Dinner. Your treat at the most expensive place in town. Eight o'clock sharp, Captain Smith's. If you're even a minute late, I'm leaving and blocking your number.

Damn. The woman decided to lay down the law, didn't she? It

47

doesn't sound like something she would say. No, if I had to guess, Everly is the kind of woman other people stomp all over because she's so nice and sweet.

"Did you hear me?" the fucker in the parking lot says.

"Yeah, later," I tell him, deciding I'm done with this conversation as I put away my phone to climb on my bike and rev the engine.

Tonight, I'll see Everly again, and hopefully I find out everything I need to know.

CHAPTER SEVEN

Everly

Taylor and I just so happened to be talking after school while letting the kids play on the playground when I got a message from Hugo.

As soon as I told her it was him, she plucked my phone from hand and messaged him back before I even saw what she typed.

Then, she called Peggy Brown to tell her to find another babysitter for tonight and tomorrow because I had plans.

There was no stopping her at that point. So, after grabbing the first dress in my closet, a spaghetti strap maxi dress with heels, I dropped off an excited Harley for her sleepover at Taylor's house and then drove myself over to *Captain Smith's Steak and Seafood House.*

When my best friend demanded the most expensive dinner in town, well, it's not high class or fancy, but at least the staff is friendly, and the food is amazing.

Once my car is parked, I sigh as I try and figure out what I'm doing here. I mean, other than Taylor making the plans for me.

I could've called Hugo and cancelled, told him I was sick or something to get out of seeing him again.

But I didn't, because...well, I'm not sure.

I guess there's still a small iota of hope that after dinner he'll sweep me off my feet and make love to me all night.

Ha! Yeah, right.

Maybe this time, I'll be the one to get Hugo all hot and bothered before leaving him high and dry.

I convince myself that it's as good a plan as any, and finally force myself to toss my keys into my handbag and get out of my car.

"Glad you agreed to see me again," Hugo says from the shadows as soon as I shut my door. I don't scream in surprise, but my heart does try to jump out of my chest. "After last night I wasn't so sure."

"Oh, um, yeah, me either," I say as I try to get myself under control. "But my best friend talked me into it," I admit as I take in his tall, sturdy frame, the cords of muscle in his arms visible even in the dimness of the dark lot. Again tonight he's wearing jeans and the leather vest with patches over a t-shirt. Not that I expected him to dress up or anything.

"I guess I owe your friend a thank you then," Hugo says.

"Guess you do," I agree, letting go of some of my animosity toward him for his rejection.

"I'm sorry if I was an asshole to you...before," he starts, as if picking up on my discomfort. "It's just, I haven't been on many dates."

I laugh at that blatant lie, but there's not even a twitch of his lips under his black facial hair. "Oh. You're serious?"

"Yeah."

"But you're hot," I say without thinking, making him crack a smile.

"Well, I don't usually date. Let's just say I'm trying something new with you," he replies.

"Why am I the special one?" I ask curiously.

He looks away from me, then takes a deep breath that lifts his wide chest. "Because you're not like anyone else."

"Yeah?"

"Yeah."

It sounds like a good thing, maybe even a compliment.

And just like that, I forgive him for rejecting me so brutally last night.

"I'm sorry if I came on too strong. That's not usually how I act," I admit as I clutch my purse to the front of my body like a shield.

It looks like a corner of Hugo's lips quirk up. "No kidding? So why am I the special one?" he asks, turning my question back around on me.

Since he was honest with me, I decide to tell him the truth.

"I haven't been on a date in about four years. My life has been crazy and hectic with work and..." I press my lips together to keep from telling him I'm raising my sister's daughter.

"And?"

I'm not a fan of lying; but if I put off the truth long enough, I might at least get a free meal before he runs away.

"Why don't we go on inside and get a table?" I suggest.

"Yeah, okay," he agrees. "But as soon as we sit down, I want you to finish what you were about to say."

Crap.

I don't agree to anything as we walk to the front doors. Hugo jumps in front of me to open the door, and then I ask Janie, the hostess, for a booth if one's available, which she promptly accommodates.

"Denise will be your server, and she'll be right over to get your drink order," Janie says as she slides our menus in front of us. Then, she smiles a few extra-long seconds at Hugo before she walks away.

I can't really blame her. The town is small, so we don't get many new people passing through, especially not hot, bearded bikers.

But Hugo doesn't even glance at her or the menu. Nope, he's staring right across the table at me, his eyes narrowed so that I can't tell if they're more golden or brown. They seem more intense than last night. Maybe that's because I wasn't looking straight at him at the bar.

"And what? What else is your life crazy with besides work?" he asks, picking right back up on our conversation from the parking lot.

I take a deep breath and try to think of something else to tell him instead of the truth, but finally say to hell with it. "And I'm raising my sister's daughter."

I brace myself for him to up and leave in a cloud of dust like a cartoon character after my admission before I even order a glass of wine. Instead, Hugo says, "Why are you raising her instead of your sister?"

"O-oh," I stammer since I wasn't expecting that response. He doesn't sound surprised that I'm basically a single mother. No, if anything he sounds...annoyed, for some reason. "Well, my sister, Felicity, she's always sort of been a wild, party girl. She didn't want to be a mother and didn't know what to do..."

"So, you volunteered to give up your freedom to be a mother to her daughter?"

"Basically. Yes."

"That was decent of you," he says.

"I love kids. Always have. Felicity knew that I wanted my own someday, so it wasn't that big of a deal for me to raise Harley instead of her." I pick up my menu and hold it up in front of my face to try and drop the subject.

"Everly?"

"Yeah?"

Hugo reaches across the table to push the menu down, so I'm forced to look at him and his serious face. "What you're doing...it is a huge deal to that little girl."

Tears fill my eyes at his gruff but certain tone. I shrug and blink them away. "I try to do the best I can for her, but sometimes it doesn't feel like it's good enough, you know?"

"Why would you say that? You give, Harley...that's her name, right?"

I nod. "I didn't know my sister was such a big DC fan. You know, Harley Quinn? But she insisted on naming her."

"Oh. Right. She was named after the comic book character," he says. "Well, ah, you give Harley a safe place to live, feed her, clothe her, right? And you obviously love her."

"Yes, but Harley is...well, she's sort of a handful, like her mother."

"She's too young to be anything like her mother," Hugo grumbles, then freezes as he hears the words out loud. "Sorry. I shouldn't have said that. I don't know her...."

"No, you're right. She's not kissing boys yet in pre-K, but she is acting out, and I am at a loss as to how to make her stop."

"Acting out how?" he asks with a frown of concern.

"Harley's teachers say she's a bully – pushing around the smaller kids, hitting them, not sharing. I dread talking to them every afternoon when I pick her up, because I know they're going to complain about something new she's done. It's like they blame me for not being able to make her behave! But how am I supposed to do that? I'm not her mother..."

"Maybe you should stop saying you're not her mother and start acting like you are."

"What do you mean?" I ask as I grab a napkin from the dispenser on the table to blot my damp eyes.

"She's young, right?"

"She's four."

"It can't be easy for her to know that her mother isn't around, and she doesn't have a father." He stops and stares at me. "I mean, I'm assuming there's no father around?"

"There's not."

"So, all of the other kids in her class probably have both parents. She's probably jealous. I know I was growing up without a mother..."

"Oh, you...you didn't have a mother?"

"I mean, I had one; she existed. She wasn't dead or anything," he clarifies. "But she wasn't around. It was just me and my dad, who was so strict I would get an ass beating and grounded if I looked at him the wrong way."

"Jeez," I say. "That sounds awful."

"Yeah, it wasn't great. I left home as soon as I graduated high school and never looked back. But enough about me," he says with a sigh. "All I meant to say is that growing up, especially when I was little, I would see how gentle and sweet the mothers were to my class-mates and I would be jealous. I guess I thought that, if I'd had a mother around, then maybe my dad wouldn't have been such an asshole. Like she would've calmed him down. I don't know. That's probably stupid."

"It's not stupid," I tell him as I reach across the table to cover the top of his hand. Only after I touch him does it occur to me that he may not want me touching him like he obviously didn't last night. Thankfully, though, he doesn't pull away.

"So, yeah, maybe your niece just wants someone to step up and be her mother for once. I'm guessing that you're great with all of the fun aunt stuff, but you might not be much of a disciplinarian."

Hearing that word, I pull my hand away and drop it back into my lap. "How can I discipline her when she's already having such a tough time? I don't want to be the bad guy, not when I'm all she has because her mother abandoned her."

"Laying down the law isn't even close to being the same as aban-doning her. It's setting her straight so that she knows what's right and what's wrong. Trust me, I had enough discipline to last ten lifetimes. Still, looking back at how I acted, if my father hadn't put his foot down with me, I probably would've dropped out of school and ended up strung out on drugs or dead in a ditch. As much as I hated it, that structure kept me in line. I'm not saying you should beat her or anything. Just maybe try and explain that when she does something she shouldn't or hurts someone, she won't get away with it. That there will be consequences."

"Consequences?" I repeat. "Like what?" I ask him.

"How the hell should I know?" he asks with a soft chuckle as he strokes his fingers over his beard and then the back of his neck. "I don't have any kids, so I couldn't tell you for sure. What worked best on me wasn't the whoopings but when I lost access to the shit I loved – my car, my phone, going out with friends. That's what kept me out of trouble. I didn't want to go without things that helped me escape my strict father."

I consider that suggestion for a few moments before I finally tell him, "Harley loves her Lamborghini."

"Her what?" he exclaims.

I laugh before I respond, covering my smile with the back of my hand. "Her battery-powered car! Not an actual Lamborghini. Jeez!"

"They have a kid's version of a Lambo?"

"Yes, and it's only a few hundred dollars. Santa Claus brought it to her last Christmas. It has real working headlights, a horn, radio, and little butterfly doors that open up."

"Oh. Okay. A kid-size car?"

"Yes, kid-sized. Anyway, Harley loves it. Whenever she goes outside, she always plays with it until the battery dies. If I forget to charge it up, she throws a fit, and I do forget sometimes..."

"So, you're going to take away her Lambo if she gets in trouble at school?"

"Yeah, yeah, I think I will. It won't hurt her."

"Just her feelings. Then, when she realizes it's her own fault for not being able to play with it and not yours, she might straighten up."

"That's a great idea, Hugo," I tell him. "I don't think about her little car that much since it's outside, but it would be perfect to hold over her. How do you know so much about kids if you don't have any?"

"I don't," he answers gruffly. "Have any or know anything about them."

"It was a compliment. There's no need to get all defensive. Besides, this is supposed to be a date, not therapy. Why don't we go back to talking about you?"

"Not much to me," he answers.

"You grew up with a strict dad?"

"Yes. And we moved around a lot because he was in the Army, which didn't help my behavioral problems. Eventually, though, by the time I got to high school, I had given up on making friends since I knew I wouldn't be around but for a few months, a year at most."

"That must have been really hard," I reply.

"It got easier the older I got."

"Is all the traveling around in your childhood why you love your motorcycle? Taking it out on the road, going anywhere you want."

"I guess so, yeah."

"And how much longer do you think you'll be staying here in Rockland with your motorcycle club work?" I ask.

Hugo strokes his beard again, his eyes looking deep in thought. "I'm not sure."

"A few more days?"

"Looks like it."

"Good," I tell him with a smile that he returns. "Now, let's order a glass of wine and some food."

CHAPTER EIGHT

Hugo

I love the way Everly smiles at me from across the table more than I should. It's probably not even me but the wine she's been downing.

This second date with her is about one thing only – gathering intel.

And I did.

Now I know that Harley is a hellion who makes Everly feel like a bad caretaker.

That sounds like someone who could very well be my spawn.

"So, I, ah, met one of your cousins today," I say to Everly to try and remind my dick that the beautiful blonde is off limits.

"Yeah? Which one?"

"Remy I think was his name? He owns the motel?"

"Oh, yeah, Remy," she says cheerfully. "He's a nice guy, although a little protective."

"Unique name."

"His full, legal name is actually Remington."

"Like the gun?"

"Exactly! His father is a gun nut, in case you couldn't tell."

"You don't say?"

"His three younger brothers are Colton, Colt for short, and Ruger, spelled just like the gun but he goes by RJ, and Barrett, who everyone calls Bear because he's big and hairy."

"Huh," I mutter. "Are they as tough as their namesakes?"

"Oh yeah," Everly replies. "They're thick as thieves and nobody in town would ever mess with them. *F with one of the Firearm Fultons and you F with all of them* has been the family motto since we were in junior high. My sister almost took it literally..." She stops talking and purses her lips. "That's awful. I shouldn't have said that about Felicity."

Taking a shot in the dark, I guess, "Your sister fooled around with your cousins?"

"I think so, once when we were all on a camping trip. I thought I heard...but all of them denied it."

"Jesus."

"I wasn't even all that surprised. When I confronted Felicity about sleeping around in high school, she assured me that she only 'did things that wouldn't get her pregnant,' which was TMI. But that's Felicity. She messed around with every single man in town before she left when she was twenty-one. Some of the women would joke and say she had to move on because there wasn't anyone left for her to flirt with or hook up with around here."

I can't say I'm all that surprised since I had hot as hell threesomes with the stripper. "And what about you? How many of the guys in town have you flirted or hooked up with?"

Everly puffs out a laugh, like the alcohol has her loosening up some. "Just one, my, ah, current landlord. We started dating when he rented the house to me. Rusty is the only 'hookup' who still lives in town. I refused to date any guys who had slept with my sister, so it was, *is*, slim pickings. The one boy I dated semi-seriously in high school moved away for college and never came back."

"You didn't leave for college?"

"Oh, I did," she says, throwing back the rest of her fourth red wine. "I didn't date much at school because I was shy and always studying to keep up my grades for my scholarship. I had just graduated with my teaching degree and moved back home when Felicity showed up pregnant."

"I can't believe she kept it," I mutter without thinking. Fuck, I guess the alcohol from the four beers is getting to me too. "Sorry. That wasn't a nice thing to say about your sister."

"No, you're right. I can't believe I talked her out of getting an abortion. She wanted to, but I promised her that if she would just carry the baby for nine months, I would do the rest. I would raise her, and it wouldn't cost my sister a penny."

"So, she had the baby and left?"

Everly nods. "Felicity lived with me rent free while she was pregnant since she couldn't strip. I think she did some of those weird fetish videos online, but that was it until Harley was born. Then, she named her and left town."

"Where did she go?" I ask, hoping I don't sound too desperate for that information.

"All over," Everly answers, which doesn't tell me a damn thing. "But for the past year or two, Felicity's been living around Vegas, bouncing from one sugar daddy to the next."

"Wow," I mutter. Vegas. Fuck. I'll never track her down there if she's not stripping.

"I want her to do whatever makes her happy, you know?" Everly says. "She's my sister. I love her, always will. It's just, I wish she would stop coming back, dropping in out of the blue and confusing Harley. "

"How often does she do that, just drop in?" I ask.

"A few times a year. Never around her daughter's birthday or even holidays. Mostly just when she's between men and needs some money."

"You give her money?"

Everly shrugs. "She's my sister. I don't want her selling her body just to eat."

"Yeah, yeah, I get that," I reply, even though it's bullshit. Felicity is a grown ass woman who could find a job where she keeps her clothes on. Instead, she takes money from her poor sister, who is already putting her heart and soul into raising her daughter.

"She's lucky to have you," I tell the woman across from me.

"Aww, you're too sweet, Hugo," she says with a real smile that she doesn't try to cover up with her hand for once.

"No, I'm not," I reply curtly.

The buzz Everly had going clears from her face when it looks like she suddenly sobers up.

Then, for a few seconds, our gazes lock and there's this...heat in Everly's blue-gray eyes like she's thinking dirty thoughts about me, which of course has me thinking them too – imagining her naked and underneath me, squirming with pleasure and begging for more. Or even better, her on her hands and knees while I'm balls deep inside of her, slamming into her from behind while pulling a handful of that blonde hair back to kiss her lips.

A few orgasms are the least the woman deserves for being a goddamn saint for more than four years.

But I'm not the man for that job.

Nope. Not going to happen. Those pleading bedroom eyes won't make me cave.

"We should probably head out," I say and have to clear the gruffness from my throat. "You know, to free up the table for someone else?"

"Oh, yeah. Right," Everly agrees. She opens her mouth as if to say something but then shuts it.

"What?" I ask as I push my chair back to get to my feet.

She lowers her eyes. "Nothing. I was just going to thank you for dinner."

"It was nothing."

"Nothing?" Everly repeats, sounding hurt.

"I meant, the pleasure was all mine," I amend, because for some stupid reason, I don't want to hurt the woman's feelings. She has enough shit on her plate. It's bad enough I rejected her last night. But how could she think for even a second that I don't want her? Any man would.

It's all I can do to not throw her on my Harley and take her back to my motel room.

"Hugo?" Everly asks, and I notice for the first time that we're both standing outside next to my bike. When the hell did that happen?

"Yeah?" I ask.

"I was just saying I hope you have a good night and that I would, um, like to maybe see you again before you leave town, if you want?"

"Yeah, I want," I agree, even if what I want is what I can't ever have.

I can't ever have Everly.

Never have neverly.

Those thoughts are funnier in my head than they should be, making me chuckle aloud. "Oh, fuck. I'm drunker than I thought," I say while shoving my fingers through the front of my hair to push it back.

"Want me to give you a ride home?" Everly asks.

I squint my eyes to examine her face in the darkness. "Do you really think you should be drinking? I mean, driving?"

"Oh. I think...I think I lost count of how many glasses I had. And I am sort of a lightweight."

"Thought so," I mutter. "The motel is close enough to walk to it. Want to sober up there with some coffee?" I offer. "The place is small and shitty, but you probably already knew that since your cousin owns it."

"Yeah, sure. Harley's spending the night with Taylor, so I'm not in a rush to get back to the empty house," Everly explains, making me freeze when I realize what that means. Her friend is keeping the kid all night in case she wanted to invite me back or she wanted to stay over with me all night.

And I just suggested we go back to my motel room.

"Nothing has to happen, except for the coffee," Everly says as if reading my mind, or my stricken face. "I promise I won't attack you or anything."

That makes me laugh again as I imagine the shy woman trying to jump my bones. Doesn't she know she's the one in trouble here? God, it would be so easy to get her out of that long, flowy dress of hers. It might cover her from chest to ankles, but a little tug on both of those thin straps on her shoulders and the entire thing would land in a black puddle around her ankles.

"I want you to attack me, really," I rush to explain as I try to ignore those crazy ass thoughts. Everly starts walking toward the motel, and I have to hurry to catch up, walking on the side of her closest to the road, even though there's not much traffic out tonight. "But, um, we shouldn't. Not with me leaving soon. You would regret it..."

"Why do you keep saying I would regret it? You don't know me that well, Hugo."

We keep walking in silence, and I don't even stumble. I could've just got on my bike and rode it the short distance and probably been fine. But that small chance that something could happen is why I didn't.

It was just the other night when I was stealing Abel's keys from him so he couldn't drive drunk.

The possibility of being a father also has me thinking about kids more than usual. Like what if I hit a car with a little kid in the back-seat and hurt them. I never really thought about that kind of awful shit before.

"Are you okay? Should I call someone to come pick me up?" Everly asks.

"No. You're good. I mean, I'm good if you're good," I stammer, sounding like a complete jackass.

"You still want to go to your motel room?"

"Yeah."

We're just two adults who have been drinking and are going to sober up in a motel room – where there is nothing to do but talk or fuck.

I really hope I'm not making a mistake.

CHAPTER NINE

Everly

As soon as we walk into Hugo's motel room, he shuts the door behind me and then there's suddenly a noticeable tension filling the air.

I mean, isn't this what I wanted to happen as soon as I felt the tingles?

The two of us met on a dating app and now we're alone in a room where a bed takes up about seventy-five percent of the small space. There's also a tiny, two-person table with two chairs, and a television on top of a dresser. That's it.

The bed is made neatly as if ready and waiting to be ravaged. Other than a black backpack in one of the chairs, the room is pretty much empty and clean. Or as clean as these old rooms get. Remy really should think about updating the décor.

I try and look for something to take my thoughts away from the warmth flowing through my veins, but there's no escaping that heat as my eyes keep going back to the king-sized bed. So, what do I do?

I go take a seat on the foot of it.

Now, it's up to him. Either he'll stay five feet away or he'll make a move. Although, he's already made it pretty clear he's not interested.

So then, why did he ask me out on another date?

God, this man is so confusing!

"I would offer you a drink..." Hugo starts.

"But there's no refrigerator?" I finish for him.

"No. I can get a soda from the vending machine, if you want?" he says, gesturing with his thumb over his shoulder to the door that's at his back since he's barely stepped foot inside.

"No, thanks. I'm fine."

"So..." he drawls. Hugo strokes his black beard as if to smooth it before slipping his hands into the front pockets of his jeans and leaning his back against the door. Okay, he's not going to come any closer.

To kill time while I sober up, I ask him, "So, how do you like living in Myrtle Beach? It's a busy tourist town, right?"

"Yeah, in the summer months, it gets crowded and pretty wild."

"And do you ever get wild, Hugo?" Okay, so my flirting sucks, but he's not giving me much to work with here.

He grins a little underneath all of that dark facial hair. "Sometimes, yeah."

That answer is not one I was expecting. "Really?"

He doesn't say anything. And after several minutes, his forehead wrinkles, and he sighs up to the ceiling looking...aggravated for some reason, like he would rather be back home or anywhere other than this room with me.

When will I learn?

He's rejected me once already. Why am I trying to make him do that again?

I don't know why he asked me for a second date, but it obviously wasn't because he's physically attracted to me.

66

Even if I was a little tipsy before, well, I'm sobering up now.

I get to my feet, clutching my purse to the front of my body. Hugo immediately straightens from his lazy slouch against the door.

"You know what? I'm feeling fine. I think I should go home now."

"Are you sure?"

"Yeah."

What I don't tell him is that I'll use the Uber app and find a ride home. Around here, we have one driver. Which makes me think it would be faster to just text Mark that I need a lift and pay him cash.

"You don't have to go yet," Hugo says.

"It feels like you don't really want me around and you only asked to be nice."

"I'm not nice," he tells me again with a gruff chuckle.

"Look, I get it. You're not interested in me that way. I wish I could figure out why you asked me on another date after last night, but I can't."

"Everly," he starts, but I shake my head.

"Could you just move out of the way so that I can leave?"

"No, not yet."

"Why not?" I ask him. "You aren't finished brooding like you would rather be anywhere else in the world than in this room with me?"

"That's not what I was thinking at all."

"You don't have to lie or pretend..."

My words are suddenly cut short when, in a blur of movement, Hugo lunges for me, his lips slamming against mine as his strong hands grab me by my hips. Then it's like the room is spinning around and around. I drop my purse to the floor in case I need my hands to keep me from falling on my face. But eventually, my back hits something so hard that I gasp against his crushing mouth.

A moment later I'm sucking in a breath for another reason when Hugo presses the entire front of his big, hard, muscular body to mine and I feel him. Like feel all of *him*.

Okay, so I was obviously wrong about him not wanting me.

Is that what this is about? He just wanted to prove that he's physically attracted to me, kiss me, and then take it all away like a horrible tease?

Why would he do that?

God, I'm so baffled I can't think straight, and I don't really want to at the moment. It's like I'm drunk on something other than alcohol as our mouths start to move together, his tongue tangling with mine, so forceful and demanding.

I've never been kissed like this before.

Not on a date. Not even in bed.

No, when I've been in bed with a man, his mouth is usually grunting above me as he jackhammers toward his release.

The kiss is hot, better than any sex I've ever had, which is sort of sad, but I push the thought away, wanting to focus on the here and now while it lasts.

Passion. That's what this feeling is.

And, wow, that whole thing about having a man get your panties wet is actually true!

Last night, I felt heat spread across my skin and a tingling between my legs.

Tonight, though, I'm slick and pulsing with need, my body ready and eager to have every long, thick inch of him inside of me.

Is that why I haven't ever enjoyed sex before? Because I've never actually been aroused and ready for it down there?

Hugo's hands that had been gripping my hips hard are now moving slowly up my sides. Doing something that seems crazy but completely necessary, I pull up my dress in one hand and grab his with the other, guiding it to where I'm hurting.

Hugo freezes a moment before he groans as if in pain. His other palm squeezes my breast while his lower one rubs me through the satin crotch of my panties. It feels so good but only for a second, until his hand leaves me. I'm expecting him to move away and put a stop to this…whatever this is. Instead, Hugo suddenly grasps my shoulders. I hear fabric ripping as he pulls and stretches the thin straps of my dress so that they can clear both of my shoulders, and then it's so long, see you later to my dress.

"Fuck. Look what you made me do," Hugo grumbles against my lips as if blaming me for the fact that I'm now standing against the door wearing nothing but a very tiny pair of black satin panties. His hands come to rest on my hips as he leans his upper body back to get a better look. The intensity in his darkening eyes scold my skin as they examine me so thoroughly while I'm practically naked.

"The panties stay on," he declares as his fingers rub underneath the thin elastic waistband.

"Then how..." Before I can even ask how we'll have sex with them still on, Hugo's mouth shuts me up, or more specifically his prodding tongue occupies every last thought in my head. That is, until one of his hands, the left one, slides around my hip and slips down to seize a rough handful of my ass.

His right hand distracts me even more when he shoves it down the front of my thong. My mouth falls open on a moan when his probing fingers find me dripping wet. I don't even have time to be embarrassed about what he'll think finding me in such a state. No, all I'm worried about is making sure he doesn't stop touching me *right there* in that perfect spot that feels so damn good.

Oh, and kissing me. He can't stop that either.

I reach up and fist his hair, fingers tangling in the soft black strands to keep his head right where it is with his tongue plunging in and out of my mouth provocatively. At some point, my leg hitches up on his hip all on its own volition.

I feel his deep rumble of sound against my chest, before his lips and tongue pull away to move lower, feasting on my neck. "You like that?" it sounds like he asks, as if he couldn't tell I'm teetering on the edge of sanity because of how his talented fingers are moving so unbelievably right against my needy flesh that I could cry. I'm not sure I could even survive at this point without just a little bit more of this amazing feeling. Just a little...bit...longer.

"If you stop before I...*OH!*" My words cut off when his hand that was on my ass suddenly moves lower and one long, thick finger penetrates my pussy from behind.

The back of my head slams against the door as an explosion detonates deep inside of me, one so intense I swear my soul leaves my body. My vision goes pitch black so I can't see anything, and all I can hear are unintelligible sounds I think are coming from me based on the burning in my throat. I don't even care, though, thanks to the sweet, addictive pleasure pulsing through every cell of my body.

The feeling lasts an eternity and not nearly long enough all at the same time before my soul floats back down to my body that's limp and useless. Thankfully, Hugo is strong enough to keep me upright as all of his fingers, unfortunately, slip free from my panties. Such a shame. I could keep them down there forever. It wouldn't take much to set me off again, just the slightest brush of his fingertips or the head of his cock before it enters me.

A shiver rolls through me at just the thought of either and both of his body parts. God, no wonder my sister is such a sex fiend, if this is what it's supposed to feel like.

"Now...I know what the...fuss is about." I either think the thought or say it aloud.

A masculine chuckle makes me think it was out loud.

When I blink my eyes open again, Hugo is crouching down to pick up the straps of my dress to bring the garment back up my body. "Can you bend your arm?" he asks when he gets to my elbow, as if I'm a small child he's trying to help dress, reminding me of all the times I had to fight to get Harley ready.

I nod, and a few moments later I'm covered again, only the baggier than normal spaghetti straps giving away the fact that the dress was yanked off of me so abruptly.

Wait. Why did he put my dress back on me before we had sex?

Hugo's palms are sliding up and down my sides and his eyes are lowered to my breasts as if he's trying to remember what's underneath or thinking about taking it off of me again. Or maybe that's just my wishful thinking.

His jeans are tented as if he desperately needs attention.

"Is it my turn now?" I ask as I hook a finger in one of his belt loops to pull him closer. He comes, brushing his lips over mine softly in stark contrast to how hard he feels against my stomach. I'm throbbing around the emptiness that I need him to fill when he backs away, no longer touching me.

Rubbing a hand over the back of his neck he turns away from me and says, "You okay to drive now?"

"Drive?" I ask since getting in a car was the last thing on my mind. It takes several long moments for me to remember why we're even in his motel room.

Oh right.

And after I promised I wouldn't attack him.

At least the attacking was all him even if I got the sole benefit from it.

"I'll walk you back to your car," he offers.

The words feel like a slap in my face. I scoff and then grab my purse from the floor to leave since he's suddenly so intent on getting rid of me. "I can manage on my own, thanks."

Turning around, I yank the door open then try to slam it closed, but Hugo is there, holding it open. When I glance at him over my shoulder, his face is closed off so that I have no idea what he's thinking about what we just did.

His piercing eyes hold mine like he wants to say something important. Instead, he tells me, "Be careful getting home. Call or text me when you get there?"

"Yeah. Sure," I agree with a puff of non-humorous laughter. I just want to get away from the confusing man before he can see me cry.

CHAPTER TEN

Hugo

Jesus. *What the hell was I thinking?* I ask myself as soon as Everly leaves. I let the back of my head thump over and over again against the same door where I just attacked her, wishing I could pound some sense into it.

Seeing that gorgeous woman standing in front of me, looking so perfect and angry, accusing me of not wanting her when it took all of my willpower to not have her right then and there made me momentarily lose my mind. She was about to leave, and I...I needed to prove her wrong and have a little taste of her mouth before I could let her go.

I gave her plenty of chances to push me away too. That's what I thought she would do when I slammed her against the door.

But she didn't.

No. She kissed me back just as desperately before grabbing my hand and shoving it underneath her dress.

As soon as I felt how wet she was, I remembered her telling her friend that she hasn't been with a man in something like four years. Then, well, I couldn't let her leave without giving her what she needed, could I?

All I could think about in those brief seconds when she was gasping and moaning from my touch was that if I didn't give her what she is begging for, then she would eventually find another man to do it. That thought pissed me off, for some goddamn reason, which is why I got her off on my fingers.

After she came so hard she could barely keep standing, she was fucking glowing. Her cheeks were flushed, blazing a pretty red from arousal and what I'm guessing was a little bit of embarrassment.

That's the moment when I nearly said fuck it all. I wanted to bury myself inside of her tight, sexy body so bad that it actually hurt – and not just in my swollen dick but all over, like deep in my chest.

The strange sensation was why I forced myself to stop touching her.

What I did was wrong. So wrong.

Mostly because now I just want to do it again, only the next time I would be using a few different body parts. One of which is trying its best to overpower all of my self-control so that I act like a goddamn teenager.

At least I stopped before I got Everly completely naked. If I had yanked her panties down her legs, then that would've been it. There would've been no stopping me from pinning her body to the wall or the bed or the floor and slamming inside of her.

She may think she wants that from me – the whole no-strings attached hookup – but she doesn't.

All of this can only play out three ways. The first is that I tell her the truth tomorrow and get the DNA test over with so I can have answers to the question eating me up inside. The second is packing up and leaving town without another word, tracking down Felicity, taking a test that proves I'm not her kid's father. The third and shittiest outcome is tracking down Felicity, taking the test that proves I

74

am the father, which means facing a pissed off Everly for the rest of my life.

If I were a smart man, I would go with option A. Hell, I nearly blurted out the truth to Everly before she left tonight, but I just couldn't. She was pissed off and hurt because I didn't fuck her, so I couldn't make shit worse.

And as of right now, well, I'm content to stay here in town a little longer, waiting around for Felicity to show back up so I can go with a new, incredibly stupid, fourth option.

I don't know why, but I want to meet the kid.

Harley.

It's not smart. I know that, and yet I have this urge to talk to the girl face-to-face, to finally make her real, I guess. Not just an idea but see her as an actual tiny, human being.

That way, I could see for myself if she looks or acts like me or Abel.

Hopefully she's blonde haired and blue-eyed like her aunt and cousins, which would make me feel more confident about the DNA results.

If I'm patient with Everly just a little longer, and we can keep all of our clothes on, well, I think I'll finally get a chance to meet the girl.

The worst that happens is Harley forgets about me, a 'friend' of her aunt who just passed through town for a few days.

But if I am her father, well, at least I won't be a complete stranger.

God, I'm an idiot.

I really should call home and let Nolan or Abel talk me out of this.

But the truth is, I don't want to be persuaded to leave. Not yet.

In my gut, I know I have to do this. I have to stay here in this small, boring town for just a little longer. It's like my internal compass that has kept me moving my entire life refuses to move an inch in any other direction. My boots are cemented to the ground, and I couldn't leave yet. Even if Roman called and told me to get my ass back for club business or he'd have my patch, Abel has my proxy if they have to take any important votes. He knows me better than anyone. So, I should be covered there.

Just in case Abel or anyone else tries to contact me, I've left my phone on silent, only looking at messages from Everly, nothing else.

Everyone and everything else can wait.

I need to do this – whatever the hell *this* is right now.

I know I'm just delaying the inevitable.

One day, I'll have to tell Everly the truth about why I'm here or leave to go find Felicity, if she doesn't turn up soon.

Eventually, one of these days I'll have to return to Myrtle Beach too. That's where my home is, my house I just bought. The roots I finally, *finally*, put down for good.

But that day isn't today or tomorrow.

Next week isn't looking good either.

CHAPTER ELEVEN

Everly

"I don't think he likes me," I tell Taylor as we sit in the chairs on my back porch Sunday afternoon watching the kids play. They're back to the game where Harley tries to mow them down in her car, which is worrisome, but Taylor doesn't seem concerned. "I haven't heard a word from Hugo since Friday night when he texted to ask if I got home alright."

"And? How did it go Friday? You didn't say much when you picked up Harley yesterday morning," Taylor remarks.

I shrug and avoid her eyes. "I thought it was a great date. We talked a lot and then afterward..."

"Yeah?" she asks, leaning in closer.

"We went back to his motel room."

Taylor gasps dramatically. "Why didn't you tell me you slept with him?"

"Shh!" I wave a hand toward the kids playing. "I didn't tell you because that didn't happen!"

"You went to his motel room and...nothing happened?"

"Something did happen, just not, you know, s-e-x," I spell out the word just in case one of the kids overhear.

"Okay, then details, please. First base?"

"Yes, first, along with a few others."

"Oooh. Was it good?"

"For me? It was amazing. I mean, he touched me, and it was like I just exploded into a million pieces. That's never happened before. My entire body went limp, and I think I passed out while standing up for a few minutes."

"So, he's good with his hands?"

"Oh yeah. And he's a great kisser."

"So, you kissed, he felt you up and felt you down. What did you do for him?" Taylor asks, now leaning forward with her elbow on her knees and her chin on her knuckles.

"Ah, that's where it got weird. He didn't...have a good time. He didn't even want me to touch him."

Sitting back in her chair, Taylor narrows her eyes. "Are you sure? Maybe while you were unconscious..."

"No. I don't think Hugo would do anything like that, and I wasn't like passed out drunk or anything. I was just resting my eyes while recovering against the door."

"Uh-huh," she murmurs.

"And it wasn't an issue of him not being able to do anything. The front of his jeans made it *very* clear that he was turned on and ready to go."

"So, he can get it up?"

"Oh, he definitely can. He was...he felt well endowed."

Lowering her voice, she whispers, "He got hard, got you off, and then nothing?"

"Yes."

"Huh. I've never known of any men who did that."

"It's odd, right? And I haven't heard from him since. Well, other than to make sure I got home Friday night."

"Now, he's starting to sound familiar. It's just, the guy usually gets a BJ or a hand job and then vanishes, never to be heard from again."

"I don't even know if he's still in town!"

"You could drive by and see if his motorcycle is in the motel parking lot. Or call your cousin, Remy, to ask. He owns the motel, right?"

"I'm not going to do either of those things! It's all too stalker-y. And if I told Remy, he would get all protective and probably scare Hugo away even faster."

"That is probably true. Want me to go by and look?"

"I'm not sure if we could even tell which bike was Hugo's. All of my cousins ride Harley motorcycles too. I mean, that's why I asked if any of them needed to be tested when Harley was born and Felicity named her."

"But thank the Lord none of your cousins were her daddy."

"Yes, thankfully. Still, we're less than a month away from the school's father-daughter dance. I don't want Harley to miss it."

"Couldn't Remy or one of his brothers take her?"

"You think I didn't suggest that to her as soon as we found out about it? She answered with a big fat no way. *'They're our cousins, Evie, not my father!'*"

Taylor laughs. "The girl definitely got her mother's attitude."

"Yes, she did. And now I'm the one who has to deal with it on a daily basis, along with her schoolteachers. I swear they just don't like her. Every day when I pick her up, they complain about something else she's done or said. She's just a little girl!"

"They get paid peanuts to watch a herd of four-year-olds. They're just overworked and tired. It's nothing personal, I'm sure."

"I guess..."

"And Harley will grow out of the behavior issues eventually. She's just trying to come to terms with being abandoned by her mother and not knowing why she doesn't have a father like every other kid in town."

That sounds similar to what Hugo said Friday night. I hate that he acted so attentive then, only to be MIA now.

Running my fingers through my hair in frustration at him and my sister, I say, "I hate that Felicity hurts her like this."

"I know. It sucks. But she'll get through it. You will too." Reaching over, she gives my knee a pat.

"Thanks," I tell her with a smile. "I don't know what I would do without you. If you hadn't been a mother two years before Harley was born, I would be so lost."

"I'm here for anything you need. Especially if you need a babysitter so you can see Mr. Good-With-His-Hands again."

"Yeah, we'll see. But I think if he was interested, I would've heard from him by now."

~

Hugo

SATURDAY, Sunday, and Monday I get up and do the exact same thing.

I pack my bag, get on my bike, and just ride, letting my Harley take me wherever it wants to go.

And every night, I end up right back in Rockland, paying for another night to stay in a crappy motel.

Then, I have a few beers and try to pass out. But I usually can't because I keep thinking about Harley.

And Everly.

I've started typing the woman a million messages before deleting them.

What the hell am I supposed to say?

I want to see you again, but we can't screw around because you'll hate me if I fuck you and then you find out I slept with your sister. And, oh, hey, by the way, could I come meet her kid to see if it might be mine?

Yeah, that won't work.

Everything I consider is either stupid or would give her the wrong idea, so I haven't said anything.

And she hasn't either.

Not that I'm surprised after how badly shit ended.

I thought she would be happy with getting an orgasm before leaving.

How was I supposed to know she wanted more? That she wanted to get me off, preferably while I was inside of her?

Now I'm fucked and have no clue what I should do since I can't make myself leave yet.

Whenever I think about Harley, memories of my childhood that I've I tried so hard to forget keep popping up in my head. Memories of brutal spankings, being locked in my room for days, constantly getting yelled at for being a fuckup.

I'm starting to think I've been putting off telling Everly the truth and getting the damn DNA test over with; because if I am Harley's father, I'm terrified of being such a shitty one that I fuck the kid up.

And from what Everly said at dinner Friday night, she's already got behavior problems and issues from Felicity giving her up.

The poor kid needs life to give her a break.

Maybe, if she's lucky, some other guy will turn up after seeing the *Meloney* show and be a decent father to her.

After all, she just wants a father to take her to the school's dance.

CHAPTER TWELVE

Everly

"Does anyone have any questions about the differences in synonyms and antonyms?" I ask before I start handing out the practice sheet to my class Tuesday afternoon. "No one? Okay, so just remember that synonyms are *same,* and antonyms are *opposites* as you go through the homework practice questions tonight."

There are some grumbles at the 'H' word that make me smile before my phone intercom interrupts and everyone goes quiet.

"Miss Fulton?" Gertrude, our front office secretary's voice blares out of the speaker.

"Yes?" I answer as I move around the room giving out worksheets.

"Mrs. Landry and Mrs. Wicker need you to come down to their classroom..."

Oh crap.

I barely refrain from saying the words out loud or an even worse swear word. Glancing at the round clock on the wall above the white board, I press my fist to my head and grit my teeth while asking sweetly, "Could you please ask them if it can wait thirty more minutes until the dismissal bell rings?"

"No, they said they're on bus duty today and a kid is bleeding."

My lungs feel paralyzed, refusing to let me take in a breath. "Harley?" I exclaim.

"No, Harley isn't bleeding," comes the exasperated woman's voice through the phone's speaker. "Harley *caused* the bleeding."

Double crap.

"I can see if Mrs. Fletcher can come stay with your class," Gertrude offers since she knows the art teacher has a free period at the end of the day.

"Okay, thank you," I reply with a heavy sigh.

"Well, it looks like you all are in luck," I turn to tell my class of second graders with a phony smile while my heart sinks in my chest. "Go ahead and get started working on your homework assignment." Grabbing my canvas tote, I load it up with papers I need to grade, along with my cell phone, then throw it over my shoulder. "If you finish up before the bell rings, then please read a book quietly at your desk. I'll see you all tomorrow," I say as I head for the door since Mrs. Fletcher's classroom is in the same hall as ours.

She's already hurrying toward me. "So sorry, Ev."

"Thanks for covering for me. *Again*," I tell her as we pass in the hallway. "They're supposed to work on their homework practice sheet and read until dismissal."

"Got it!" she says before I turn the corner to hurry down to the pre-K classroom, dreading this meeting while also ready to get it over with.

Mrs. Landry is standing just outside the classroom door, arms crossed over her chest, the toes of her sneaker practically tapping impatiently when I see her. Sitting on the floor on one side of the hall is Harley, with her elbows propped on her knees, her palms cupping either side of her face – the picture of patience.

On the floor next to Mrs. Landry, though, is a brown-haired boy with ruffled hair holding an ice pack on his head, tears still running down his face.

"What happened?" I ask when I reach them out of breath.

"This one," the teacher starts, pointing a finger at Harley, "tried to give Elliot a haircut."

"Oh no!" I exclaim, already picturing the disaster with scissors before their teacher kneels down and moves the ice pack from the boy's head to show me the small, bleeding wound.

"She cut a few snips of his hair and a chunk of his forehead!" Mrs. Landry shouts in outrage. "His mother is going to go ballistic when she sees him. Then I have to be the one to tell her what happened, and she's going to blame me!"

"Well, you are their teacher," I remark. "If they had scissors out, they should've been closely supervised."

"There are sixteen kids in our classroom, Miss Fulton. I can't keep my eyes on that one every second of the day!" She points her finger at Harley again, pissing me off with the way she keeps referring to her without using her name.

"Harley?" I kneel down in front of her, and she raises her chin stubbornly. "What were you thinking?"

"It's his fault!" Now it's her turn to point her small finger. "Elliot asked me to cut his hair for him because it was too long and kept getting in his eyes!"

"You can't cut someone's hair even if they ask you to do it, okay? People have to go to school to learn how to cut hair before they can do that for other people."

She shrugs. "It would've been a good cut if he hadn't turned his head!"

The teacher grumbles something and says, "Just take her home. I'll give Elliot's mother your phone number so she can yell at you later!"

Getting to my feet, I offer my hand to Harley to help her up. She takes it, and I ask, "Where's your backpack?"

"In my cubby."

"Can she go grab it?" I turn around and ask her teacher.

"Make it fast."

"Grab it so we can go," I tell Harley as I put my arm around her shoulders to urge her forward. "And tell Elliot you're sorry you cut him."

The teacher helps the boy up, but like most kids this age, Harley follows my directions in the order I gave them, walking right past him, back into the classroom. When she returns a moment later with her LOL Surprise backpack strapped on, she throws her arms around the little boy and even kisses him on the cheek.

"I'm sorry you didn't stay still like I told you to when I cut your hair."

"Harley!" I exclaim at the same time the teacher groans. "Harley, sweetheart, you can't blame him for your mistake. You cut his skin and made him bleed!"

"If he hadn't moved, I wouldn't have cut him!" she exclaims before she spins on her heel and takes off running toward the exit.

"I'm so sorry, Elliot. I hope you feel better," I say as I start to chase after her. "I'll apologize to his mother too!" I tell her teacher before I have to turn and full out run to catch up with Harley before she goes out the door into the parking lot where buses are already pulling up.

I grab her hand to stop her, pulling her up short before she steps off the curb.

"You can't run away from me like that!" I tell her. "You could've been hit by a car or-or a bus!"

"You get mad at me for everything!" she shouts and tries to pull her hand away from mine.

"No, I don't get mad at you. I just get frustrated. Harley, stop trying to run off before you fall down!"

As if on cue, she drops to her knees, squalling at the top of her lungs, refusing to budge from the sidewalk.

"You know scissors are only supposed to be used on paper and crafts even if he asked you to give him a haircut," I explain even though she probably can't hear me over her own wails. "So, tonight, you won't get to ride in your car or watch TV."

Her fake sobs cut off so abruptly it's like I flipped a switch.

She looks up at me with sad, puppy dog eyes, her lashes actually wet with tears and lower lip jutting out in a pout. "No...car?"

"No car tonight or TV," I repeat.

"But...but..."

"No, Harley. No excuses. You cut your friend with scissors and hurt him."

All the fight finally goes out of her, so I easily scoop her up and carry her on my hip to my car.

Her sniffles are quiet as she rests her head on my shoulder, breaking my heart because I hate seeing her upset. But something has to change before she cuts a kid's ear off or ends up in juvie by the time she's thirteen. Okay, so I'm probably being a little overdramatic with juvie. I know Harley can be a sweet girl who can follow the rules; she just...doesn't like to most of the time.

"If you don't get in any more trouble at home tonight or at school tomorrow, then you can drive your car tomorrow and have thirty minutes of television, okay?"

Her head nods in agreement before I open the backseat of the car and get her buckled into her booster seat.

Before I shut her door, she looks up at me and says, "I'm sorry, Evie."

"I know you didn't hurt Elliot on purpose," I tell her with a smile as I smooth her dark hair back from her forehead.

Her face brightens. "So can I play with my car when we get..."

"No!" I answer with a shake of my head. "Not tonight. Your friend got hurt even if it wasn't on purpose. You broke the rules with the scissors. There are consequences for breaking rules to teach you what's right and wrong so that you won't do it again. Do you understand?"

Her lower lip comes out even further as she crosses her arms over her chest, but she doesn't scream or cry on the way home.

In fact, she's a perfect angel, getting her bath without putting up the usual fight about not wanting to get her face wet. Then, she eats all of her dinner, even her peas and carrots without complaint.

I'm thinking a tantrum is coming any second like the three or so she has most nights, but then I'm tucking her in, reading her two stories twice each and telling her goodnight.

"I really hope you'll follow all the rules tomorrow for your teachers," I say.

"I will. Promise," she says before I kiss her cheek and turn out the light.

"I love you, Harley. Even when I have to fuss at you or take things away, I still love you and don't want to have to do any of that," I assure her.

"Does my mommy love me even when she's not ever here to tuck me in?" she asks.

"Yes, of course she loves you," I reply as I blink back tears. "Everyone who knows you loves you."

"My teachers don't," she mutters.

"They do love you. That's why they have so many rules to try and keep you and your friends safe while you're at school."

"Oh," Harley replies. "What about my daddy?"

"W-what about him?" I ask as my heart drops to my stomach.

"Does he love me even if I've never seen him?"

"Yes, he loves you too," I tell her, because sometimes a lie is better than the truth – that her father is out there in the world with no idea that she even exists.

CHAPTER THIRTEEN

Hugo

W hen I woke up Wednesday morning, I told myself this was
it, that I was going to leave town once and for all and just
call back the *Meloney* show to schedule the damn paternity test.

I took my key back to the motel's office and turned it in and told
the woman at the desk I was finally checking out.

Feeling like I was doing the right thing, I walked outside, climbed
up on my Harley... and then the sky opened up.

There goes that plan.

By the time I can trudge back into the office to pay for one more
night, get the key, and return to my room, I am completely drenched.

The weather app on my phone never even showed a chance for a
pop-up shower!

Since my clothes are soaking wet, I take them off and throw them
over the tub to dry while I take a hot shower, debating for the

millionth time if I should send Everly a message or not before I leave tomorrow.

Maybe I should and that's the reason why the rain kept me here for another night.

I even make up my mind on what to text her, *Want to hang out tonight?* It's the least ridiculous thing I could come up with before I turn off the shower and start drying off.

That's also when there's a knock on my hotel door.

Worried it could be housekeeping coming to clean, thinking I've left, I quickly wrap the towel around my hips and use my right hand to hold it as I go answer it before they bust in on me.

But when I open the door, it's not someone pushing a linen cart but a beautiful blonde. Today, Everly is wearing a short, flowing, blue dress with baggy sleeves that make her eyes look more blue than gray and a pair of black heels that have her legs looking sexy as hell.

"Oh, wow," Everly mutters. While I was staring at her, she's been looking at me. Her eyes are fixated on my bare, damp chest before they lower to my abs, stopping on the towel.

"What are you doing here?" I ask, surprised to see her and questioning if she's really here or it's just another dream I'm having starring her.

Her pink lips part as her mouth falls open before she goes up on her toes to see over my shoulder into the room.

What is she...oh, she thought I might have someone in here with me?

That would be funny if over the last four days I hadn't considered finding someone, anyone to bring back to my room to try and fuck Everly out of my system.

The motel clerk would probably have been up for it, but I didn't ask. Couldn't, for some stupid reason.

"Did I...am I interrupting anything?" Everly's fingers are fidgeting with the foil-covered plate in her hands. Wait. When did that get there? Has she been holding it the entire time? I must have missed it thanks to her sexy legs and pretty lips pulling all of my attention to them.

"No, you're not interrupting. I was just getting out of the shower," I tell her. Opening the door wider, I clear my throat and say, "You can come in if you want."

"Oh, so there's no..."

"No what?" I ask.

"Nothing," she replies with a dismissive wave of her hand as she slips in past me so I can shut the door. "I'm sorry to come by unannounced. I made you this." She holds out the plate to me, and I take it awkwardly with my left hand since the right is trying to keep my towel in place.

"Ah, thanks. What is it?" I ask, turning around to go sit it on the wobbling two-person table so I can subtly adjust my thickening cock behind the thin cotton.

When Everly doesn't respond, I turn back around to face her and say her name.

Her face lifts from the part of my body the towel is covering, her cheeks going pink. "Huh?"

"What did you make?"

"Oh, right. That's, um, cheesecake brownies."

"Cheesecake brownies?"

"Yes, I hope you like cheesecake and brownies. They don't have to go in the fridge or anything," she rambles.

"Okay. Thanks." Still keeping one hand on the towel, I run my fingers through my hair to push it out of my face and then over my soggy beard, wishing I knew why she was here with baked goods after how things ended Friday night. When she doesn't say anything more, I ask, "What did I do to deserve homemade cheesecake brownies?"

"You were right."

"I was?" I say in surprise.

"Yes." Everly pulls her purse around in front of her, using it as a shield like she's done every time I've been with her.

"About what?"

"Harley."

Just hearing her name is a gut punch because I really wish I could meet her. Clearing my throat, I ask, "What about her?"

"I took your advice after she got in trouble at school. Well, first I asked her *why* she cut a boy's forehead with scissors before I went straight to apologizing to her teacher. And then, even though I could sort of sympathize, I punished her."

"She cut a boy's head?"

"Yes. Made him bleed and everything."

"Why-why would she do that?" I ask in concern, worried that Felicity and I could've made a monster...

Everly puffs out a bark of laughter. "She was giving him a haircut!"

"Oh. That's not so bad."

"I know, right! She's not a bad kid," Everly rushes to say in Harley's defense. "She wasn't thinking. He asked her to cut his hair so it wouldn't be in his eyes, and then he moved..."

"So, it was his fault?" I remark.

"No. Maybe. Harley knows she's not supposed to use scissors on anything but paper, so she had to apologize and take responsibility. Even if she basically blamed him in her apology."

Smart girl since she's right. "She's four and was just trying to help what sounds like a friend. Knowing better, making better decisions, especially when it comes to going along with friends, doesn't come until later in life."

"Yeah, I guess not," Everly replies. "Although, I still find myself having decision-making issues at my age," she admits as her bluer than gray eyes roam down the length of my body again in obvious appreciation.

"I should, um, probably get dressed," I say.

"You don't have to..." she trails off, causing me to arch one eyebrow in question.

"Everly..." I have to stop encouraging her, hell, I know that. I guess I just like that she wants me, even though she shouldn't.

"Don't say we shouldn't or that I'll regret it," she blurts out as if reading my mind.

"You will," I assure her, but she's already shaking her head in disagreement.

"No, Hugo. I've thought about you all weekend and the past few days no matter what I was doing. The only thing I'll regret is if you leave before we have a night together."

I groan and scrub my hand over my face since I've done the same thing. In fact, wasn't I going to text her after my shower, knowing that if she agreed to hangout something more would happen between us?

This woman, she's going to be the death of me, strutting into my motel room looking like a gorgeous dream with her long legs and pretty lips, making me hard as hell while she stares at me like she's starving for what only I can give her.

I'm not sure why she wants me. If I told her the truth, that I slept with her sister years ago, several times, with another guy, and one of us could be her niece's father, well, she would fucking loathe me.

I should tell her all of that right now to wipe that longing off her face.

I don't, because it would kill a piece of me to hurt her, someone so sweet and sad and beautiful.

I shouldn't lead her on by letting this go any further. Hell, I know that. But if I turn her down again, that will crush her too.

So, I decide to go with the lesser of two evils.

I'll give in. Give her what she needs while torturing myself with no relief in sight. I don't deserve an ounce of pleasure for putting her into this situation.

If I don't put on some clothes soon, though, well, I won't be able to help myself.

Boxer briefs won't cut it. They're too soft and easy to get off.

That's why I pull the clean, dry jeans from my backpack, pulling them up my legs, button them, zip them, and secure my belt.

There.

It would take at least ten or so seconds to undo all of that again, enough time for me to come to my senses before I bury myself inside of Everly.

Hopefully.

~

Everly

HUGO GROANS, his forehead wrinkles in thought, then his palm scrubs down his face. I have no idea what any of that means in grumpy biker language.

"You're going to be the death of me," he finally says after he puts on a pair of jeans.

"I guess I can take that as a no," I remark with a heavy exhale as I turn around and start for the door.

"Everly?"

God, I hate that I love the way my name sounds on his lips.

"Yeah?" I ask, my hand on the doorknob.

I expect him to make more apologies or excuses about why this, us being together is a bad idea. Instead, Hugo finally says, "Are you sure you want this?"

Like he even has to ask.

"Yes," I answer softly without turning around, unable to move a muscle as I hear him approaching me. I'm suddenly nervous and unsure only because I dread what comes after, him telling me to leave, not seeing him again. "I want this, but only if you do. I don't want it to be out of pity or anything else..."

Hugo's strong hands grab my shoulders, spinning me around so that I'm facing his broad chest.

"How could I not want you, blondie? You're so fucking beautiful." Without another word, he takes both of my wrists and pins them above my head on the door before his frantic lips lower to cover mine.

I only get a brief kiss compared to the last time before his mouth moves down to my neck. Transferring my wrists to one of his big hands, the other grabs the hem of my short dress and starts pulling it up my body, over my head, and then he releases my hands to remove it from me entirely. Like usual, I didn't need a bra, so I'm only wearing a pair of lacy, sky-blue panties.

Those are frantically tugged down my legs. Hugo's warm, calloused palms stroke up my thighs until they get to my bottom where they grip my cheeks roughly and lift me up the front of his body. The new position makes it easy for Hugo to open his mouth to take an entire breast into it and suck. Hard.

"Oh my god!" I exclaim, my head falling back on the door, eyes slamming closed as a shiver runs all the way through me. I need pressure between my legs, but I can't even close them now that they're in his tight grip. "Bed, please!" I plead as I cup the sides of his head, running my fingers through his hair. I want to feel Hugo's heavy weight bearing down on me. I need him inside of me so badly that I don't even mind begging. I'm so beyond caring about things like pride or dignity. There's nothing but the hands and mouth of this man driving me crazy.

Of course, the stubborn biker doesn't listen to me.

But his mouth does keep moving lower or my body keeps rising higher up the door, I'm not sure which. Maybe both.

When I'm able to open my eyes again, I realize I am being lifted higher up the door, but I'm not scared of him dropping me. His muscular arms aren't even trembling the least bit as they quickly reposition one at a time to hook around the insides of my thighs, spreading them wider as his lips and tongue trail down my stomach. Hugo's facial hair is both incredibly soft and abrasive on my skin. I love the combination that's so...*him*. I don't know if I'll ever understand what's going on inside this confusing man's head. How could I possibly be mad at him now, though, when his warm, wet mouth is pressed to my inner thigh, oh so close for where I'm desperate for it.

There's not the least bit of shame in me when I tug on his hair to guide him those few inches to the right. I hear his gruff chuckle right before the first swipe of his tongue runs through my folds, parting them, causing me to make a loud, shouted moan of surprise.

"You like that, blondie? Those beautiful golden locks are all natural, huh?" it sounds like he asks. I answer by arching my back and pressing his face to my body, needing his tongue to keep licking me right now instead of trying to have a conversation about the color of my hair down there.

His laughter turns into a groan when he swirls his tongue into my opening and shoves it deep inside of me until I feel the tip of his nose rubbing against my clit.

I scream his name but relax my grip on his hair in case I'm smothering him. Hugo doesn't retreat, though.

The muscles in my thighs tighten and tremble with the need to move, to have his tongue deeper, higher, faster. But his fingers are gripping me so firmly they may be leaving bruises.

"Hugo, please!" I exclaim as I get closer and closer, needing just a little more pressure on my clit.

Finally, his tongue finds the spot again, making me cry out.

"Right here?" he asks.

"Yes, yes, yes!" I chant with each of his rough, wet flicks.

And then I'm soaring higher than my body or even the sky as I'm overwhelmed by the pleasure so intense the shudders may rip my arched spine apart.

For a moment, it's like I'm seeing Hugo and I from the ceiling, his face pressed between my legs as he lifts me to nearly the top of the motel door. I've never even thought about doing something so erotic.

God, it feels so good I don't want this feeling to ever end.

But all too soon, my backside is sliding down the door, and then I melt into a puddle of skin and bones on top of something...soft.

I blink my heavy eyelids open. At first, all I can see is the top of Hugo's black hair, then I feel his lips as he kisses his way up my body until his face is right above mine.

"You...that was..." I try and find the right words that seem so far away. Then, I remember Hugo putting on his jeans before he kissed me. He knew then what he intended to do. "You're not going to let me touch you, are you?" I ask him.

"No," come his firm response even though his golden-brown eyes look a little desperate and...hungry.

Yet again he's being so...soft but abrasive. I want to understand this man, but I'm not sure if I ever will. Still, right now, I don't want to try and think about his rejection too hard.

When I reach up to grab the sides of his face, pulling his mouth down to mine, he thankfully comes. His lips are soft against mine, and I'm the one who prods his open to swipe my tongue over his, tasting myself.

It's certainly different. Everything with Hugo is different. He's the first man who has ever gone down on me. Or did I go up on him since he lifted me up the door to his mouth?

I laugh, and Hugo pulls away, staring down at me with one thick eyebrow arched in question.

He wants to know what I was laughing at, but instead I ask him, "Did that feel like I regret anything?"

His heavy sigh blows over me before he says, "Maybe not tonight, or even tomorrow, but one day..."

I press my finger to his lips to stop him. "Hugo?"

"Yeah?"

"Will you shut up and cuddle with me for a little while, or do you think I might regret that too?"

The biker grumbles something under his breath before he stretches out beside me and throws his arm over my waist.

"Thanks."

I expect some smartass remark telling me I'm welcome, but instead he says, "I was going to leave today, before the rain..."

"I'm glad you didn't," I say, refusing to ask if he's leaving tomorrow if the sun comes out. Instead, I roll to my side and get comfortable as the big, bearded man presses himself against my back, his manhood so hard against my bottom that he must be hurting. God, he's so stubborn. I wish I could figure him out.

CHAPTER FOURTEEN

Hugo

I get no sleep. None at all.

I lie in the shitty motel bed with an arm around a naked Everly, who breathes so loudly in her sleep some would even consider it snoring.

Still, I don't dare move other than to pull the covers over top of us.

I just lie there as still as possible trying not to wake her. And eventually, maybe three hours later, my dick finally, thankfully, gives up on getting any relief.

I deserved every second of the ache.

And I already know that tomorrow I'll be too damn tired to ride home.

I mean, I could probably handle it, but I would feel like shit, which means I'll be staying in town another day.

While I lie there awake, I can't help but notice just how different Everly and I really are.

She's beautiful and shy with light eyes and hair, sweet and selfless while I'm grouchy and loud with dark features, being completely selfish for keeping up the charade with Everly that we're dating.

It's so wrong and stupid that I have no doubt I'm going to hell for hurting her.

When she finds out the truth, she'll hate me, which will suck either way but especially if I'm Harley's father.

I may even hurt her so bad that she never lets me near the girl. Then I would only have myself to blame.

No matter how unexpected this whole thing is with Felicity and Harley, the last thing I want is to not be a part of her life if the tests say I'm responsible for bringing the kid into this world.

Especially not after seeing how frustrated Everly is for having to pick up the slack for not just one absent parent but two.

So that's it. Tomorrow, I'll finally leave, go back home to Myrtle Beach, and wait for Reece to track down Felicity.

But then I hear the raindrops on the windows and roof of the motel room and know that I'm lying to myself.

Everly

I WOKE UP AROUND SIX-THIRTY, right when the sun would've been coming up, if it wasn't a cloudy, rainy day.

Hugo was out cold, so I quietly got dressed and slipped out into the yucky day, needing to shower and get myself and Harley ready for school.

Oh, and apologize to Taylor for staying out all night.

That's not what I intended.

100

I thought I would enjoy a few minutes of being held by a man before I got up and left. Instead, I fell asleep for not just hours but the entire night!

At least Hugo didn't wake me up and tell me to leave.

Maybe he would have if he hadn't fallen asleep too.

The house is dark and quiet when I creep in the back door, my wet heels squeaking on the kitchen linoleum.

Still, I don't wake up Harley or Taylor. At least not until my closet door creaks as I open it to find clothes for the day.

"Oh, hey," Taylor murmurs. "You're home."

"I'm so sorry for keeping you here and for not calling."

"I was hoping you were enjoying yourself and hadn't been kidnapped or anything," she says as she sits up and wipes the sleep from her eyes. "Hope you don't mind I crashed in your bed."

"No, not at all," I assure her.

"So? Does this sneaking in you're doing mean your date went well or you escaped the kidnapper?"

"Ah, it was a pretty good date, but I really need to hop in the shower. You can head home if you want. I know you need to get the boys ready for school."

"And I know you're trying to get rid of me," Taylor says as she throws the covers off and gets out of bed. "I want details later."

"Absolutely," I assure her with a smile. "How was Harley?"

"That girl was a perfect little angel. Not a peep from her all night. I had to check on her a few times to make sure she was sleeping; I just couldn't believe how well she acted."

"Good," I say with a sigh.

Taylor pulls on her pants while saying, "I, ah, heard about her cutting a kid from Carson."

"It was an accident!" I exclaim. "Really. She was just trying to cut his hair."

"Oh," my best friend remarks. "And he moved his head, didn't he?"

"Yep, that's what she said."

"Have you ever tried to cut a four-year-old's hair? It's freaking impossible. It's a wonder she didn't cut his ear off."

"Oh, god, I can't even imagine," I say as I rub my forehead. "At least his mom didn't sound ready to sic the town with their pitchforks and torches on Harley. She just said to ask Harley not to try any other haircuts in the future on the boy."

"She's not as bad as you think she is, Ev," Taylor says while slipping on her shoes.

"Yeah, but when she's bad, there have to be consequences. I know that now."

"Good. Because every kid is going to try and push limits once and a while."

"Right," I agree, hoping she's telling the truth and not just trying to make me feel better.

"Do you want me to stay while you shower?" she offers.

"Nah, Harley will probably sleep until I wake her up at seven."

"Okay. Well, details later?"

"Sure thing," I agree, even though my face starts to burn just thinking about the night before.

"Ooh, it must be good if you're blushing like that!"

"It was," I reply with a smile.

"That's great. I'm so happy for you, Ev." Taylor throws her arms around me for a quick second, and then she's gone.

THE SCHOOL DAY goes by in a blur, mostly because it was a rainy day, so all my kids looked sleepy and were content to watch *The Magic School Bus* for the last hour of the day.

Meanwhile, I kept getting distracted by flashbacks of last night with Hugo. The way he tasted and felt, how strong and dominating he had been holding me up on that door, how amazing it felt, and how I want to do it all again with him.

I was cool and calm after school when I went to pick up Harley from her pre-K class, not even stressing when her teacher brought her out.

"Have a good afternoon!" Mrs. Landry says as she urges Harley out to the hallway. Then she turns around and starts to go back inside.

"Wait!" I call out. "How...how did things go today?"

I look down at Harley and then back at her teacher, who actually smiles. "No problems to report."

"None?"

"Not a one. Harley was on her best behavior again today. If she has a third day in a row tomorrow, then she'll get a prize from the prize box."

"Oh, wow, that's so exciting!" I say to Harley when her teacher walks away. "Are you excited?" I ask as I take her hand in mine and lead her back to my classroom to grab my things. I know she's never got a prize before or she would've mentioned it.

"Yeah, I guess," she replies. "Don't know what's in it, though."

"Well, you'll find out tomorrow."

"Yeah," she says. "It's probably something stupid like a pencil or eraser."

"What do the other kids get out of it?" I ask.

"I don't know. They pull a prize out on the way out the door."

"Oh," I mutter. I understand why the teachers would wait until the last part of the day, so that the other kids won't be jealous of the prizes if they don't get one. But at the same time, if it was something fun and Harley knew about it, she may have had more incentive to behave. Not that bribing kids is the best way to encourage them to follow the rules and behave. Still, it usually works with the little ones.

I'm still smiling in the car all the way home as Harley sings along with the Kid's Bop CD. It's amazing how one little good thing can make you feel lighter. Not having to worry about whether or not her teachers hate her is a load off my shoulders.

And, yeah, I think I'm still feeling the euphoric effects of the orgasm from last night. Not to mention that, since it's been raining all day, it's a safe bet that Hugo hasn't left town yet.

Everything seems to be going great, until we get home and find a river flowing from the bathroom into the hallway

"Fu-udge sticks!" I exclaim when I see the growing puddle.

"What's wrong, Evie?" Harley asks from behind me.

"Stay back, sweetie. The bathroom is flooding. Can you grab some towels from the laundry room?"

"Uh-huh," she says with a nod before she takes off.

While she's gone, I quickly remove my shoes and socks, roll up my pants legs, and then wade into the bathroom to figure out what's causing the flood. As soon as I see that its water pouring down from the ceiling like our own personal black cloud lurking above us, I wince and hurry back to the kitchen to find some pots since I don't have any buckets.

"Crap, crap, crap!" I groan as I get soaked when I line up the two pots, then run out of the bathroom as fast as I can once I realize there's not a bucket big enough to catch this downpour.

Harley is standing at the edge of the newly formed river holding a single towel in her hands, bless her heart.

"I promise that I didn't do this, Evie," she says with a slight lisp that shows up whenever she's nervous.

"Oh, sweetie, I know you didn't do this. This is all from a hole in the roof that's nobody's fault. We'll call the landlord, and he'll get it fixed in no time."

"Are you sure?" she asks as I tiptoe out of the water and head straight to the kitchen to grab a towel to mop up my dripping face and hair.

"I'm sure."

"It just feels like everything is all my fault," her tiny voice says sadly from beside me.

"That is definitely not true," I assure her while drying my hands on a towel. "You know I didn't like taking away your car and TV time, right? That I only did that because you misused your scissors on the boy at school. That's all it was for. Nothing else."

"Okay," she says with a nod.

"How about we grab you a snack and then turn on cartoons while I get the bathroom fixed up?"

"Okay."

She heads for the living room while I grab an apple juice box and a small bag of Goldfish. Once she's all settled watching *Paw Patrol,* I finally pull out my phone from my purse and call my landlord Rusty from the number in my speed dial.

The house is cute but old, so it's had a lot of issues since we moved in five years ago. But it had a fenced-in backyard, three bedrooms, and was within my budget, so I snatched it up.

I make a sound of aggravation when Rusty's voicemail comes on, then wait for the beep.

"Hey, Rusty, it's Everly. I'm sorry to bother you, but this is an emergency! That stain in the bathroom ceiling that I told you about months ago is now a big hole! Rain has apparently been pouring into the bathroom all day, so now the bathroom and hallway are flooded. Please call or come over whenever you can and fix the roof! Thanks."

Ending the call, I try and figure out where to even start with the cleanup. I'm not sure if I have enough towels to mop up that much water. Besides, what's the use if it's going to keep on raining for a few more hours.

I'm still holding the phone in my hand, debating whether or not to call Hugo. I don't want to seem like a clingy woman after he gave me a few orgasms, but I think he would know what to do, how to fix anything. He just has that whole, hot, handyman vibe going on. So, before I can talk myself out of it, I pull up his phone number and call him.

"Everly?" he answers. Good to know that he's saved me in his contacts, I guess.

"Hi, Hugo. I'm so sorry to bother you. In fact, you may not even still be in town. You may have left in the rain…"

"I'm in town," he answers.

"Oh, well good," I say in relief. "Then, ah, maybe would you consider helping me? I have sort of an emergency situation."

"What's wrong? Are you okay? Is it Harley?" he asks in a rush.

And, wow, I'm surprised he remembered her name. I couldn't have mentioned it but once or twice when we were talking about her getting into trouble at school.

"Everly? Answer me, woman!"

"Oh, sorry. And yes, Harley and I are both fine. It's my roof."

"Your roof?" he repeats in confusion.

"The roof has had a small leak, but now it's opened up to a big hole, so my one and only bathroom flooded while we were gone today!"

"Flooded?"

"Yes, there's water everywhere, even out in the hallway, and I don't even know where to start until the roof is fixed, and my landlord didn't answer his phone!"

"I'm on my way," he says without any hesitation, making my shoulder slump in relief.

"Thank you so much, Hugo!" I reply before he ends the call.

Only after I hang up the phone do I realize that I never gave him my address and he didn't ask for it. So, I shoot off a quick text while biting my bottom lip.

I didn't want to have random men coming over while Harley was here, but this is a dire situation. It's not like I'm inviting him over to have dinner with us or introduce him as my boyfriend or anything.

Harley probably won't even notice he's here.

I grab more towels, clean and dirty ones from the laundry room, and then I start trying to soak up the water, making my way to the bathroom.

At least we don't have carpets, or they would be ruined.

Still, there is so much water. It looks like it's going to take forever to get it all up.

CHAPTER FIFTEEN

Hugo

E verly invited me over to her house.
   Only because her bathroom is flooded, but still I'm finally getting my chance to meet Harley up close and personal to see if there is any resemblance to me or to Abel.

What if she doesn't like me? is my first thought as I get off my bike, drenched all the way to my bones. Riding my bike was quicker than running over here or waiting for a lift. I jog up the steps to rap my knuckles against the front door.

There's no more time to stress because the door opens and standing on the other side is not a tall, beautiful blonde but a little girl with jet black hair and big brown eyes, looking up at me like I'm ten feet tall instead of a little over six. She's...nothing like I imagined. I thought she would be blonde since I know Felicity dyed her hair black. Instead, she's got dark hair like me and Abel.

"Who are you?" she asks while cocking a hip and resting a hand on it, reminding me so much of Felicity. It's definitely the attitude she got from her mama and not her sweet, overly trusting aunt.

"Hey, ah, I'm Hugo."

"What do you want?"

"I, um, your aunt Everly called me and told me about the bathroom. Mind if I come in?"

"Hold on," she says just as I start to take a step forward, slamming the door in my face. And, damn, if I don't hear her turning the lock on the other side too.

Smart girl.

She doesn't know me. It's a good thing that she wants to go get Everly for her approval before letting me in their house.

A moment later, the door is jerked open again and I come face to face with an exasperated Everly. Her long, blonde waves are pulled up into a messy bun on top of her head. Her black dress pants are rolled up to the knees and her pink button down has the sleeves rolled up to her elbows.

"Oh, thank goodness!" she says, sounding so relieved at the sight of me that it makes me want to kiss her. But no, that's stupid.

"Come in. Sorry about Harley."

"No, it's fine. In fact, it's great that she's so careful of strangers."

"Yeah, well, she has trust issues."

"Sorry..." I start, but Everly just waves her hand dismissively and motions for me to come inside.

"I've started trying to soak up some of the water, but I feel like it's pointless because more keeps replacing it," she tells me as I follow her through the living room where Harley is now sitting on the sofa, her legs dangling and kicking. She continues facing the television like I don't even exist. I refrain from staring or stretching my neck too far. I really want to see her face again, but not creep her out.

When we get to the bathroom, I quickly see the problem.

"This isn't so bad," I assure Everly. "Got any tarps or any pieces of wood to cover it with? A hammer and some nails maybe?"

"Ah, yeah, I think there is a sheet of that, um, plywood or whatever in the shed in the backyard, along with some tools and maybe a tarp."

"Okay. I'll go take care of covering the hole, then we'll work on cleanup."

"Yeah, okay," she agrees with a burst of laughter while wringing her hands. "Oh god, it's such a huge mess!"

"Not for both of us. We'll get it cleaned up quickly together."

"I'm sorry you have to deal with all of this and get even more soaked in the rain. I called my landlord and left him a message but..."

"It's fine, Everly. I don't mind getting a little wet."

She looks away at that comment, and I think her cheeks flush.

Oh, is she thinking about how my mouth got her soaking wet last night?

Fuck, well, now I'm thinking about that too.

"Do you have a wet/dry vacuum?" I ask her.

"No. But maybe Taylor's husband Kyle has one I can borrow. I'll go call her."

"Okay."

I follow her out of the room trying to avoid the deeper puddles, even though there's not much that can do damage to my shitkickers.

"The shed is out this way," Everly says as we walk through the living room. I still don't get another good look at Harley. The girl is good at avoiding eye contact.

"I'll be right back," I tell her before I head out into the rain.

"Be careful!" she calls out, making me smile because she's worried about me falling off her roof.

I LUCK up and find everything I need in the shed, including a ladder, to do a quick patch on the roof. I knew the damn thing looked old as fuck the first time I saw it. It should've been replaced years ago; and if the landlord doesn't get it done soon, more of those holes are going to open up and ruin everything Everly owns. The woman is lucky that it was just the floors and not any furniture this time.

Since no one had a wet/dry vac, I borrowed Everly's car to go and pick one up at the local home improvement store and told her to go make dinner or something since there was no point trying to mop up that much water. I could tell the usually calm hippie was getting more and more frustrated by the second.

An hour later, with the biggest wet vac the store owned, and the place looks almost as good as new.

"Wow," Everly says from behind me in the hallway right after I shut the vac off. "You got it all up?"

"Yep."

"Thank you. I don't know what I would've done if you hadn't come over. The whole house would probably be flooded by now."

I turn around to tell her that's the fucking truth, since her landlord was no goddamn help. But when I see her, the words evaporate. "You changed clothes," I remark like a real Einstein.

Everly glances down at her tight, white tank top and short gray shorts as if noticing them for the first time when we both know she picked them out intentionally. If she was trying to tempt me into fooling around with her again, well, it's working thanks to those hard nipples pointing right at me, begging for my mouth. Then there are her long, sexy legs on full display thanks to the shorts that are small enough to classify as panties.

"I thought I might have to help with cleanup," she says, which is bullshit. "Anyway, um, dinner is ready if you're hungry."

Hungry doesn't even begin to describe what I am. I've had my hands on her, my mouth on her, and haven't allowed myself any relief since the first night we met, not even in the shower. It's a form of cruel and unusual punishment that I think could break even the strongest of men. Does the military know about this sort of pain? If so, I'm surprised my father never used it on me.

"Hugo? Do you want to come eat with us?"

Us, right. Her and the girl that could be my own flesh and blood.

"Ah, yeah, I could eat," I reply, and again Everly's cheeks flush. I'm starting to think I could say anything, and it would get a rise out of her.

I shouldn't like that idea as much as I do.

"Do you want a change of clothes? I could put those in the dryer for you."

Now it's my turn to glance down after forgetting my t-shirt, jeans, and socks are soaked. I took off my cut before I went to the shed to save the leather. If I looked in the mirror, I probably resemble something like a soggy dog. The wet weight of the denim on my dick is all that's keeping the bastard in check.

"A shower and some dry clothes would be great."

"Not sure if I have anything that will fit you well, but we can at least find something dry," Everly says before she disappears through a door that I'm guessing is her bedroom.

I finish tidying up the bathroom, taking an armload of wet towels to the laundry room next to the kitchen. The smell of pork chops hits me right in the gut, making it growl.

It's followed by a girly giggle.

Harley is standing right outside the laundry room in pink footed pajamas, a plush cat tucked under her arm and a smile on her face. She looks so sweet and innocent that I can't figure out how Felicity could just leave her.

"Your stomach sounds funny, like a mad doggy," the girl says.

"Yeah?"

"Yeah."

"Doesn't your stomach make the same sound when you're hungry?"

She scrunches up her nose in thought for a second before shaking her head no.

"Then you're lucky." When I was her age, I remember sitting in my room starving with the gnawing ache in my belly, wishing I had a bite of anything to eat. Withholding meals and beatings were my father's usual punishments for pretty much everything when I was a

111

kid. It was so infrequent to have three meals a day that I still sometimes forget to eat more than one even though I'm in my fucking thirties.

Harley tilts her head to the side while eyeing me up and down. I've never felt so judged by anyone in my entire life. So, when she opens her mouth to speak, I have no idea what she's going to say.

"Can you dance?"

"Ah, what?" I ask.

"Dance?" she repeats, and then she wiggles her hips back in forth in demonstration.

"Can *I* dance? God, no."

Her face falls as if that's the wrong fucking answer before she says, "That's too bad."

"Hugo?" Everly calls out just as she steps out of the hallway and finds us standing in the kitchen. "Oh, there you are. I put a shirt and some sweats in the bathroom, along with a dry towel."

"Ah, thanks," I reply. "And, um, the food smells good."

Everly smiles at me as she goes to the table and pulls out a chair that Harley hops up into. "We'll snack on rolls and save the main course for when you join us."

"You don't have to wait."

"Well, we won't wait all night, will we, Harley?" she asks while smoothing the little girl's dark hair back over her shoulders.

"Nope."

"So, you better hurry," Everly adds as she grabs the foil pan of rolls from the counter and sets it on the table.

Since I'm looking forward to a homecooked meal after days of fast food, I hurry.

CHAPTER SIXTEEN

Everly

"Is that man your friend, Evie?" Harley asks a few minutes after Hugo goes into the bathroom.

"Yes, he's my friend, and his name is Hugo," I answer.

She sounds out his name slowly between bites of her roll, her plush calico cat named Cutie Pie tucked under her arm. I don't think it's a coincidence that it's the same thing Felicity calls Harley on the few occasions she comes to visit. "Does Hugo's name start with an H like my name?"

"It does," I agree with a smile. "H-U-G-O is how you spell Hugo."

"He's big," she says around a mouthful. "And his hair is black like mine."

"Don't talk with food in your mouth, sweetie. You could choke," I warn her as I push a cup of water toward her. "And, yes, Hugo is big and has black hair."

She makes a big show of swallowing the bite of roll in her mouth, then "There's a lot of hair on his face too."

"Some men have facial hair like Hugo's called beards."

Thankfully, that's the end of her questions as the two of us put down half the rolls before Hugo finally comes stomping back into the kitchen, stopping behind the chair next to Harley's at the dining table. The first thing I notice are his bare feet, which look gigantic. The navy-blue sweats that are too big on me fit him fine, just a little short, although my gaze lingers on the front longer than it should when I realize he's probably going commando underneath. When my eyes finally lift to the t-shirt, well, Harley giggles and a similar sound pops out of my mouth before I slap my palm over it.

"Shirt is a little small," Hugo says unnecessarily since we can obviously see that.

The white *Friends* tee is stretched so tight across his broad chest that it's practically see through. His biceps are straining the short sleeves as far as they can go and probably leaving an indention in his skin. But the best part is the bottom hem that comes to about halfway down my thighs stops just above Hugo's bellybutton that's surrounded by hair the same black as the ones on his head and beard. It's pretty ironic that he looks as ridiculous as Ross from *Friends* when he put on the *Relax* shirt.

I remove my palm from my mouth to tell him, "Sorry. That's the biggest shirt I own."

"You look silly!" Harley informs him.

"I know I do, but I'm too hungry to really care," he says as he pulls out the chair and sits in it.

Getting up from the table to fix him a plate, I try not to laugh at him again, but it's difficult.

Still, instead of getting annoyed, Hugo just looks resigned to his fate while we have dinner.

He digs into his pork chops and corn salad like a starving man, only pausing long enough to grab a roll here and there.

Harley eats most of her plate too without complaining that she would rather have a peanut butter and jelly sandwich or a plain grilled cheese. That's usually what she asks for every single night while I try and get her to try a few bites of vegetables.

"What's for dessert, Evie?" she asks before Hugo is finished eating since that's always her favorite part of dinner.

"Strawberries and a little whipped cream."

"Yes!" she exclaims. "I'll get the whip cream."

She runs to the refrigerator and opens the door to grab the spray can while I grab the container of strawberries to start washing them.

"Hugo, do you want any strawberries?" Harley asks when she takes the can back to the table.

His eyes widen in surprise that she called him by his name. "Ah, no thank you."

"Fine. That leaves more for us," she tells him with a grin as I bring the strawberries to the table.

"Does your little cat there like strawberries?"

Harley scoffs. "No! Cutie Pie is not a real cat. And real cats don't eat strawberries."

"My mistake," Hugo says, his palms raised in surrender, his hazel eyes filled with humor as they meet mine.

When Harley stares at the man the entire time she's eating her strawberries, barely dipping them in whip cream, I know she's thinking deep thoughts. So, I'm not even all that surprised when she says, "I want Hugo to read me a story at bedtime tonight."

"Hugo may not be able to stay that long tonight, sweetie," I say before he has a chance to answer, giving him an easy out.

"What time is bedtime?" Hugo asks.

"Seven-thirty," Harley answers.

"I could probably stay that long and read a story," he responds. "If that's okay with *Evie*." A grin curls his lips under his facial hair when he uses her nickname for me.

"That's, ah, fine, yeah," I answer since I was hoping he would stay. Not just to read a bedtime story to Harley but to maybe tuck me into bed too.

My face warms at the sudden, naughty turn in my thoughts. I get to my feet and say, "I should probably grab your clothes and throw them in the dryer."

∾

"Turns out there was enough cupcakes for everyone," Hugo finishes reading and then closes the book.

I'm about to tell him one of us has to read it again as per the usual routine when Harley sighs, her eyes growing heavy as she tucks Cutie Pie under her chin and says, "I like when everyone gets a cupcake."

Hugo's brow furrows while he strokes his beard and hands me back the book. "Ah, yeah, that's pretty cool to make sure there's enough."

"Thanks, Hugo. Goodnight."

"Night," the biker replies.

"Do you...don't you want me to read it again or read a second book?" I ask Harley.

"No. Night, Evie."

"Oh. Okay. Goodnight," I reply as I lay the book on the bookshelf, then slowly back out of her room, motioning with my hand for Hugo to follow me.

Once we're in the hallway, I turn off the light and shut her door.

"Wow," I whisper.

"What?" Hugo asks. "Did I fuck it up?"

"No, you didn't 'eff it up'," I assure him with a smile as I grab his wrist and pull him across the house to my bedroom where I shut and lock the door behind me before resting my back against it, letting out a sigh of relief.

"Usually, I have to read two books twice, at least. Sometimes more," I explain to him. "And it's not that I mind reading to her, it's just that by the end of the day I am wiped out, you know?"

116

"Yeah, I get it," he says. "You're working all day and raising her on your own. Not to mention minor roof emergencies."

I groan and bury my face in my hands. "It's always something, you know?" Dropping my hands, I say, "Thank you for coming to help, and, um, for staying."

Hugo glances away, then reaches up to run his palm over the back of his neck. "It was no big deal. Do you think my clothes are dry yet?"

"They probably have a few more minutes," I lie. "Why? Are you in a hurry to leave now?"

His eyes meet and hold mine a second before he says, "Not really, no, but I figured I should go so you could get some sleep."

"I'm not really tired yet." Unlike most nights, I'm suddenly very awake knowing I'm alone in my bedroom with a really hot man for the first time in so, so long.

"No?" Hugo asks as his gaze finally, thankfully, lowers to my breasts like maybe we're getting on the same page.

I don't have to look down to know my nipples are hard and poking through the thin fabric of my tank top.

But I don't want to give this man a chance to distract me before I finally get my hands on him for once.

"If you're staying a little longer, can I thank you for helping me out tonight?" I ask as I just go for it and grab his waist with both hands, touching that yummy-looking skin he's been showing all night thanks to the small shirt.

"You already have thanked me," Hugo says as his heavy exhale blows through the top of my head.

"With words, yeah, but not with actions." I slip my fingers down into the elastic waistband, brushing them over his happy trail and... oh, yes, as my hand strays lower my fingertips graze the base of his thick cock. My hands retreat, gripping the material at his waist with both hands as I glance up at his face for permission.

Hugo's eyes are more golden than brown as he stares down at me with a familiar hunger filling them.

Since he doesn't knock my hands away, I sink down to my knees, pulling the sweatpants down as I go. His cock that I've only felt and never seen is even bigger than I imagined, long and veiny and a little overwhelming. I'm pleased to see he's already getting hard as it bobs a few times once freed. I wrap my fingers around the thick base, unsure where to even start. I finally swipe my tongue over his slit before attempting to take him in my mouth. Instead of a grunt or groan of pleasure, Hugo says, "Ev, wait."

When his hands come down and roughly squeeze my shoulders, I assume he's getting ready to pull me back to my feet and stop this from going any further.

Instead, he tugs on the spaghetti straps and shoves them down my arms. When they get to my elbows, I pull each of my arms free just as Hugo jerks the front of my tank top down to reveal my breasts.

The next time I grab his thickness, he groans as if in pain and his cock jerks, hardening even more.

"Now?" I look up at his face to ask him.

He nods wordlessly before leaning forward to brace his forearms on the bedroom door and resting his forehead on them as he stares down at me.

Happy to finally have him on board with this, after what has felt like an eternity, I release his cock to run my hands up his hairy, muscular thighs, wanting to tease him a little like he teased me.

I let my thumbs graze the inside of his thighs, brushing his sac before sliding my hands down and back up a few more times. Then, I move upward to his hips, pushing the tight tee up to reveal more of his abs. I run my fingernails down those etched muscles.

"Ev, please," Hugo begs quietly. "I need...need your mouth, blondie, and you fucking know it, don't you?" His voice is deep and growly as if he's in pain before his hips punch forward, rubbing his dick across my cheek. "You're fucking killing me."

I tease him one last time, running my tongue along the length of him before finally fisting him and guiding his crown between my parted lips.

Hugo's long, drawn out gasp of my name makes every time he rejected me before now well worth it.

I'm certain that he's wanted me, wanted this the whole time but was holding back for some strange reason. I knew I wasn't crazy; that he was just being stubborn when it's like a switch is flipped and his hips begin thrusting, unable to move in and out of my mouth fast enough.

"Oh, fuck me. Being in your mouth is even better than I imagined."

His distressed curses and grunts are music to my ears as he finally takes what he needs from me.

The back of my head bangs against the door a few times before Hugo's cock is pinning me to it, taking complete control and fucking my mouth frantically. His fists slam on the wood above me as his face and upper body are pressed to the door as if he can't get close enough or deep enough.

"Fucking heaven," he says before his cock hits the back of my throat, making me gag once before he eases up just as I taste the first hint of his salty flavor on my tongue.

From somewhere miles away I hear what sounds like a doorbell ringing, then pounding. I assume it's Hugo's fist above me until he finally reaches down to grab the back of my head and says, "Don't care who it is. I'm too close to stop now."

Each word is a forceful pump into my mouth.

When I unfortunately gag again, Hugo pulls all the way out. "Sorry..."

There's more banging, sounding louder this time, making me wince as I remember we're not the only ones in the house.

"They'll wake up Harley. Fuck," Hugo grumbles before I can say the words. When he pulls up the sweats, tucking himself under the elastic waistband, I snap out of the lustful haze and scramble up off the floor.

"Who the hell is coming over this late at night?" Hugo asks me as I try and fix my top.

CHAPTER SEVENTEEN

Hugo

I'm not sure if I'm more relieved or aggravated about having someone interrupt us.

It's a good thing, because sooner or later I'm going to have to tell Everly the truth, and then she'll be glad that she never fucked me.

She'll regret wrapping her lips around my cock, but I can't say I will. All I regret is that I didn't get to finish. Having her on her knees, a saint looking like a sinner, well, she was so damn gorgeous.

But she can't be mine no matter how badly I want her.

"Who the hell is coming over this late at night?" I ask Everly as I hurry and put my dick away, feeling something else along with the confusing lustful emotions. Protective? Yeah, I think that's the one. This is just the one night I'm over here. Everly and Harley are home alone all the other nights. It's not safe for them, no matter how small and safe she thinks the town is.

"I-I don't know," Everly replies as she tries to get her top back in place. Then there's some other feeling bubbling up inside of me now.

Jealousy.

Was Everly lying about not dating anyone else? Does she really not know who is showing up so late? I've made a lot of assumptions about a woman I barely know.

"I'll take care of them then," I say when I decide to go answer the door myself.

"Hugo, wait! It might just be Taylor."

In the hazy fog of lust, it takes a few moments for me to remember that Taylor is her friend's name. In this case, it's thankfully a female's name I think, not a man's.

I didn't bring my gun inside with me, which I now regret. It's locked in my saddlebag since I didn't want to have that around Harley or scare Everly.

Now, though, I'm wishing I had it in my hand. Especially when the goddamn doorknob turns, as if the person on the other side is either breaking in or has a fucking key.

Hoping to catch them off-guard, I yank and pull the door open hard to reveal a tall, skinny man as he stumbles forward.

"What the fuck do you want?" I bark at him.

He staggers back a step as he visibly shakes himself. Then his eyes narrow at me and quickly fill with a loathing so fierce I *really* wish I had my gun. "I'm Rusty, and I own this house. Who the hell are you?"

His question comes out caustically, making him sound more like a jealous boyfriend than a landlord. And I hate to admit that the asshole isn't anything close to ugly, unfortunately, with his blond curls and clean-shaven face.

When everything was hectic, I think Everly said she had called him to fix the leaking roof but had to leave a message.

"You're a shitty fucking landlord," I inform him as I turn my asshole level down from a ten to an eight. I want to tell him he has no right to come inside, but if it's his house...I guess technically he can even if it's wrong.

"And you look like an idiot," he retorts, gesturing with a hand at my clothes.

Ignoring his jab, I tell him, "The entire bathroom and hallway flooded today because you're too fucking cheap to replace the roof."

He opens his mouth to respond, then closes it before asking, "Where's Everly?"

When he tries to walk past me, I sidestep to get in his way and press my palms to his chest, shoving him back toward the door.

If I thought he looked and sounded angry before, it's nothing compared to the wrath oozing out of him now. "Keep your fucking hands off of me!"

Before I can respond, Everly steps in between us, so I take two steps back, my clenched fists relaxing.

Turning to face the landlord, she says, "Sorry, Rusty. I wish you would've called me back earlier when the place was flooded."

"I did call you back! You didn't answer!" he exclaims angrily.

"Shh. Keep your voice down. Harley's already gone to bed," she reminds him.

"He was coming in even if you didn't answer the door," I point out.

Rusty's jaw clenches before he says softly, "I'm sorry to bust in, I just got worried about you when you didn't come to the door." The fuming asshole attitude he had when he barged in is gone quicker than you can snap your fingers.

"Well, I'm fine, and Hugo put a temporary fix on the roof and got the water cleaned up," Everly tells him.

"Oh. Okay."

"She needs a new roof," I mutter. "When are you going to replace it?"

Ignoring me, he tells Everly, "I'll call and get some estimates for the roof this week."

"Thank you," she says.

"The front door could use some paint too," I point out.

"Hugo," Everly says in warning.

"I can work on that too," the jerk assures her. Then he looks from her to me and back again. For the first time I notice exactly what he's seeing – Everly's face is flushed, her lips red and swollen from sucking on my cock. I can't believe I let things get that far. Hell, I lost control and even treated her like a whore, making her choke on my dick.

"Guess I should leave you to it," the asshole says.

"Yeah, thanks, Rusty," Everly replies as he thankfully turns around and walks out. She shuts the door and locks it behind him while I quickly try to figure out what the hell to do.

"Ah, I should probably get going too," I tell her when she turns around.

Her more gray than blue eyes widen in surprise. "But you didn't...I thought we would finish what we started."

"It's getting late," I point out even though I'm not tired. Everly mentioned being exhausted at night, so the best thing I can do is let her get some rest instead of confusing her even more.

"Are you sure?" she asks.

"Yeah."

Everly's eyes lower, reminding me I'm still in her shirt and sweats.

"I just need to grab my clothes from the dryer and change."

Since I know where both of those things are, I go to work, getting dressed in the bathroom where I think for a few seconds I may have to get Everly to cut off the tee before I manage to finally get it off.

"Here you go," I say when I hand the sweats and tee back to her and shove my feet in my boots.

"You're really leaving?"

"Yep."

Everly follows me over to the door with the clothes in her arms. Glancing outside through the window, I'm happy to see the landlord fucker is long gone.

Tomorrow, I'll put new locks on the door to make sure he can't barge in on Everly and Harley again.

"Thanks again, for everything," Everly says as I open and walk out the door.

"No problem," I tell her. When I reach my bike and she's still standing in the doorway, looking so damn good I want to pick her up and carry her to bed, I tell her, "Lock up behind me," to make sure I don't change my mind.

The door shuts a little harder than was necessary, making me think she's mad at me again.

The woman is pissed because I wouldn't let her finish me off with her mouth?

Yeah, there's no one else like her in the world.

It's too bad I fucked her sister years ago, screwing up any chance the two of us might have had if I were the type to settle down.

Which I'm not.

I mean, I have settled down, back in Myrtle Beach where I bought a house. I remind myself over and over of that fact as I ride back to the hotel.

The whole town is dark and sleepy other than a well-lit garage, both bay doors wide open, several motorcycles parked out front.

Since I'm sure as shit not sleepy, I slow down and turn into the second entrance to pull around the place to back my Harley in next to the others.

I'm second-guessing dropping in on strangers just because we have a common interest when I kill my bike and hear a familiar voice say, "Colt, man, you are so full of shit!"

Remy.

At least I sort of know the asshole who runs the motel, so I climb off my bike and walk around to the open doors.

Inside the garage are several guys, all tall and well-built with tats on their arms and various shades of blond hair like some sort of golden biker boy cult.

"Hugo! Hey, man!" Remy says in greeting as he strolls up to me with a bottle of beer in his hand. "What the fuck you doing out here?"

"I didn't mean to barge in on anything," I tell him.

"It's a garage. You're not barging in, although we might put you to work," he jokes with a grin. "Come on in and meet my idiot brothers." I follow him further inside where the guys all gather round, well, except for the one who is on the ground working on a bike. "So, the one as wide as he is tall is the youngest – our baby brother Barrett. The dude covered in grease on the floor is RJ. And this fucker next to me is Colt."

The guys all lift their chins in greeting but don't offer to shake hands.

"Nice to meet you. Sorry for busting in. I saw the bikes out front and lights on, so I thought I would stop in."

"Hell, we're just drinking a few beers, tinkering with RJ's ride, and shooting the shit. What are you up to?" Remy asks.

"Nothing much." Instead of talking about being at Everly's, I try to quickly change the subject. "Nice rides ya'll got here."

"Thanks, yours too. Saw it at the hotel yesterday," the one named Colt says. "The special edition Fatboy, yeah?"

"Yeah."

"Those are hard to get your hands on. How did you pull that shit off?" RJ sits up and asks from the ground.

"Ah, yeah, back home in Myrtle Beach, the Savage Kings own the local dealership, so we get all the good hookups."

"Sweet," the bulky one, Barrett, remarks with a big smile.

"College girls all summer and banging rides? Must be nice," RJ grumbles before he goes back to the wiring on the headlight assembly he's holding.

"There are some perks to living in a busy tourist city. But it still gets cold and lonely in winter."

Nodding his bottle of beer toward me, Remy asks, "So what exactly are the Savage Kings all about? Are they a one-percent club?"

"You mean part of the one percent of motorcycle clubs that are outlaws who do whatever the hell they want? Not really, at least not without a damn good reason." I shrug and tell them, "Sometimes the right thing is the wrong one in the eyes of the law, but it still has to be done."

"Yeah, we get that," Remy replies.

The five of us spend the next hour or so talking about rare bikes and sports or whatever. And when there's eventually a lull, I decide to ask them, "What do you all know about that Rusty guy in town?" I almost say 'Everly's landlord' but figure there's no reason to admit to her cousins that I've been going over to her place. "You know, the curly blond bastard?"

"Oh yeah, we all know Rusty," Colt replies. "He's an odd fucking dude."

"How so?" I ask since I got the same impression from his sudden mood swings.

"Remy, you went to school with him, didn't you?" Barrett asks his brother.

"He was several years older than me, way too old for the girls he always tried to date."

"How much older?" I ask.

"He was thirty going after high school girls back then," Remy says. "Then his parents died, leaving him a ton of cash, so he bought up a bunch of real estate. The asshole doesn't have to earn a living like the rest of us. He just sits back and collects rent..." Remy narrows his eyes at me. "Why are you asking about him? You hot for him or something?" he jokes, and the other guys laugh.

"No, not that there's anything wrong with that," I reply defensively because they have me thinking about Abel. "I just ran into him, and he was kind of a prick."

"That sounds about right," Colt agrees with a chuckle.

"Well, hell, I better get on back to the motel," I tell them. "Nice meeting the Fulton Four."

"Have a good one," Barrett says.

127

"Stop by whenever you want," Colt calls out. "We're here about every night."

"Those of us who can't get laid, you mean," RJ jokes, making them all laugh.

Remy doesn't say goodbye but follows me out to my bike. "So, how long are you going to be staying in town at the motel?"

"Not sure," I answer as I put my helmet on and fasten the chin strap.

"Then we'll keep charging your credit card every day until you leave," he says. "And if you hurt my cousin, you won't be able to ride that pretty bike of yours."

I'm a little surprised it took him this long to threaten me if he knew I've been seeing Everly. But then I guess everyone knows everything that goes on in this small town, especially after she came by my hotel room. Twice.

"Yeah, I know," I assure him.

"Aren't you going to tell me you won't hurt her?" Remy asks.

"Can't promise anything."

"Then don't fuck with Everly. It's as simple as that, man."

"No, it's not. I wish it was that easy, but it's not," I tell him before I crank my bike and drive off.

In fact, I can't stop thinking about Everly or ending up being with her. It's almost like the world is scheming against us — the rainy days bringing us together over and over again, stopping me from leaving and causing the leak at Everly's so that I had to go and help her tonight.

Or maybe that's just the bullshit I'll keep telling myself when I don't get on my bike and leave for good tomorrow.

CHAPTER EIGHTEEN

Everly

After Hugo's sudden exit last night, I didn't have high hopes of hearing from him Friday. Still, that didn't stop me from constantly checking my phone for messages whenever I had a break.

At least the school day went by fast since the kids had the fire department visiting and they were excited about the weekend.

"Did you like seeing the firetruck today?" I ask Harley on the ride home.

"Uh-huh."

I wait for her to say more from where she's buckled in the backseat, but she doesn't. All of the kids in my class were so excited about getting to climb up in the trucks, try on the gear, and then they each received a red plastic fire helmet to take home. Almost every student leaving the school at the end of the day had their hat on, but Harley's is smushed into her *Doc McStuffins* backpack.

"You didn't want to wear your cool new hat?" I glance up at the rearview mirror to ask her.

"Nope."

"Why not?"

"Do you think my daddy is a firefighter?" Harley asks out of the blue.

I focus on the road in front of me as I try and figure out how to answer that question. My policy is to always tell her the truth no matter what because she already has trust issues with Felicity coming and going, and I want her to trust me. "Ah, I-I don't really know, sweetie. I guess it's possible..."

"Colby's daddy is a firefighter. He gets to drive the big truck."

"Oh, well, that's exciting," I remark.

"Colby said he's going to be a firefighter just like his daddy when he grows up. Evie, what am I going to be if I don't have a daddy?"

I deflate in the driver seat and nearly miss the turnoff for our road. My foot hits the breaks harder than usual to slow down in time.

"Harley, you can be anything you want to be when you grow up, even a firefighter. You don't have to pick the same job as your parents."

Please don't let her ask me what her mother does for a living. And please, god, don't let Harley follow in Felicity's footsteps.

"In fact, I bet a lot of kids miss out on exciting careers if they limit themselves to only doing what their dad does," I assure her.

"What was your daddy, Evie?" Harley asks. When I glance at her in the mirror, I see her gnawing on her bottom lip. She does that whenever she's thinking too hard about something.

"My dad was, *is*, a poker player," I tell her honestly. "That's someone who foolishly bets money on a game of cards."

"And you didn't want to be a poker-er?" she asks, adding an extra *er* to the word.

"No, I did not want to be a professional poker player. I wanted to be a teacher because I like working with kids. I went to college and worked hard to get my degree so that I could teach."

"Did my mommy go to college?" Harley asks just as we pull into the driveaway.

"No, she –"

"Hugo is here! And he's got a big bicycle!" she exclaims.

I'm thankful for her distraction and to see the man in the leather vest and jeans sitting on my porch steps. He stands up as I put the car in park, and then Harley is hurrying to get her seatbelt off like she's happy to see him too.

I hear her pulling on the doorhandle that I keep locked, just for times like this when she's ready to bolt without thinking about other cars and traffic.

When I finally get out and open her door for her, she takes off running to the biker. For an instant, I worry that she might hug him, and he won't reciprocate it, pretty much like he does with me.

Not only does Hugo hug her back, but he also swings her up and puts her on his hip.

"What did I do to deserve such a greeting?" I hear him ask her before he looks over at me approaching them. "I haven't even showed you your surprise yet."

"A surprise? For me?" Harley exclaims, her jaw gaping in shock. I think mine might be too.

"Hopefully your Aunt Evie won't mind?" Hugo asks as he grins at me.

I stare at the usually grumpy and closed-off bearded biker, wondering if he got a personality transplant overnight. I mean, if he had actually got to finish in my mouth, then I would maybe understand his new and improved mood, but he left here annoyed and frustrated.

"I should've asked you first, right?" he says.

I have to shake my head to clear away the images of us last night to focus on the present conversation. "What's that?"

"Her surprise? I should've asked if it was okay with you first, shouldn't I?"

131

"A heads-up would've been nice, yes," I answer while pushing my hair behind my ears. "But, um, I'm glad you're here."

"Show me! Show me! Show me!" Harley says, her patience wearing thin as she kicks her feet, narrowly missing Hugo's crotch. He grunts and quickly puts her down as if thinking the same thing, then whispers to her loudly, "It's in the backyard."

"The backyard? How did you..." I start to ask.

Hugo pulls a keyring from the front pocket of his jeans and holds it out to me. "I changed your locks. Hope you don't mind. I just didn't like knowing that creepy bastard from last night could come inside whenever he wanted."

Wouldn't he have had to break in to change the locks?

"What's a bastard?" Harley asks, making me wince.

Hugo mouths the word sorry to me, then tells Harley, "It means not a nice person."

"Oh."

"It's not a nice word, and you would get in trouble for using it at school or at home," I warn her. "Like big trouble, losing your car trouble."

"Okay," Harley huffs. Placing her hands on her hips, she asks, "Can we go to the backyard now?"

"Yes. I'll come back for your backpack later," I agree as I pass by Hugo to climb the steps and try out the shiny new keys. That's when I see there's an extra lock above the old one.

Behind me, Hugo clears his throat and says, "I also added a dead-bolt. Can't believe you didn't have one. And a chain. I mean, that's the least a woman living alone should have on her door."

"Thanks, but it wasn't necessary. Rockland is a safe town," I tell him as I get both locks turned so we can go into the house.

Harley speeds past me and runs right to the backyard where she too easily works the new deadbolt and lock on it to yank the door open. She's out the door a second later, making me even more thankful for the fence. Then I hear her scream.

Or I should say squeal, since it's most definitely a happy sound.

"What did you..." I turn to ask Hugo before Harley is back, grabbing my hand. "Come see, Evie! It's a bicycle like Hugo's."

"Motorcycle or bike, not bicycle!" Hugo corrects her from behind us. "And they're called Harleys, just like your name."

As soon as I step into the screened porch, I spot the tiny electric pink and black motorcycle.

I must have stopped walking because Harley is tugging on my hand once again to get me moving out of the porch, down the steps to the flat yard.

"It's named after me?" she asks while throwing her leg over the seat to hop up.

"That's right," Hugo tells her.

Harley puts her foot down on the pedal, and then she's gone.

"You bought her a bike?" I say in disbelief as she cackles while doing donuts around me and Hugo.

He strokes his beard as he watches her with a grin. "Uh-huh."

"And put it together and charged it up today?"

"Yep."

"Why?"

That question finally has his eyes lifting to mine. "Are you mad?"

"No. I just...I can't figure you out."

Stepping closer, he whispers, "She's been good at school, right? Doing better?"

"Yes, but..."

"She loves it. The site said it's made for ages three to six. Oh, and I can get her a helmet if you think she needs it. Should've thought of that before now honestly, but I haven't spent much time around kids."

"Hugo, this is too much!"

"It's nothing."

I give him a look that says he's so full of crap. The motorcycle had to have been a few hundred dollars, not to mention the shipping to get it here overnight, and the time it took to put it together. Again, I want to ask him why since his response doesn't make sense.

"Now you've got another bargaining chip for when she misbehaves, right?" he asks.

"Uh-huh."

"You're pissed at me," he says.

"No, I'm just, I don't know what I am."

Harley begins to stop and start the bike abruptly, over and over again, making her head whip forward and back as she giggles, loving every second of it. And seeing her happy, well, of course that's all I want for her.

"Thank you. I guess I should've said that before giving you the third degree."

"It's okay. I should've asked you first," he says as he rubs the back of his neck. "I need to get going."

"You're leaving?" I say in disbelief. How is he going to drop this bomb on us, doing something so sweet I want to cry and then just up and leave? "Don't you want to stay for dinner? It's Friday night, so we usually do takeout."

"Yeah, Hugo! Stay for dinner!" Harley says as she circles around us again, throwing up dirt and grass.

"Maybe next time," he says to her, which I know is his way of letting her, us, down easy.

"You don't have to go. I'm not angry. How could I be?" I ask as I wave my hand at Harley with her new favorite toy.

"There's...somewhere I have to be. Nothing personal," he mumbles. But whenever someone says that phrase, it's *always* personal.

Before I can call him on it, he's already walking toward the porch, heading up the steps. "Oh, and I patched up some of the worst spots on the roof to hold you until you get a new one."

"You did?" I ask as I glance up, noticing a few jet-black shingles here and there. They don't match the others that are all faded to gray thanks to years of the sun. Not that it's a problem with the new pieces not matching. As long as there's no more flooding inside the house, the entire roof could be bright yellow or pink polka dotted for all I care.

"Thank you," I tell Hugo again.

But when I look back down at the porch, he's already gone, his bike revving up from the front yard.

What in the world is up with that man?

CHAPTER NINETEEN

Everly

I don't hear from Hugo at all Saturday, no texts, no calls, no impromptu visits or gifts. He's gone radio silent again like last weekend.

And I'm not the only one who notices his absence.

"Where's Hugo?" Harley asks as we eat her favorite dinner – spaghetti with meatballs, because it's so messy. "Why didn't he come see me ride my new bike?" Her lower lip sticks out in a pout, and great, not only is he disappointing me but also her. This is why I knew it was a bad idea to invite him over when the roof flooded the bathroom. I should've waited on Rusty to come fix it. But I'm glad it was Hugo and not the landlord. Now I just have to figure out a way to explain why he may not come around again.

"Well, um, Hugo is just a friend. You don't see your friends every day, do you?"

"No," she replies as her fork pokes around at her spaghetti noodles. "When will he come back?"

"I'm not sure."

"But I miss him!"

"You do? You only met him a few times."

"I miss mommy, and I've only seen her a few times," Harley counters. And since that's so freaking sad and there's nothing I can figure out to say, I decide to change the subject.

"How about a Disney movie tonight with some popcorn if you take a quick bath?"

"Okay!" Harley agrees, her face brightening at the mention of two of her favorite things, which even overshadow the horror of the bath.

During the entire one hundred and three minutes of *Moana,* I'm distracted, trying to figure out how a man can be so sweet and then so distant. I can't figure out if he likes being with me or not, but then I consider the things he's done, fixing the roof and changing the locks, buying Harley a Harley, and I don't think he would've done those things if he didn't care.

And then there's the physical things we've done, which I thought were the hottest of my entire life. He's definitely not using me for sex since we haven't had any. What man doesn't let a woman finish getting him off?

If he doesn't want to see me again, I'll live. I know that. I just want to know where we stand so I can stop obsessing about him.

After I read Harley her bedtime story, just one story once since Thursday night when Hugo read to her, and tuck her in, I go to my room and lie down in bed to try and figure out how to just ask the man for clarification. Are we going to see each other again or not? If not, then he's a jerk for involving Harley, giving her an incredible gift, and then disappearing.

Is he even still in town? It hasn't been raining since Friday morning, so he could've left last night or today.

I'm afraid that if I text him a question, he'll just ignore it, making things worse.

I hate this feeling of being toyed with and wish there was a way to even the score between us.

There's one way I could try to get his attention by text message, and it doesn't involve any questions.

I've never done anything like it before, though.

I've never even *considered* doing anything like this even once. And maybe that right there is the problem, why men don't find me sexy or irresistible. I never step out of my comfort zone to try to be sexier.

With Hugo, though, I'm attracted to him in a way I've never felt for anyone else, so I want him to want me too.

Even if I have to do something that makes me a little uncomfortable like sexting him.

If I'm honest with myself, it's not a bad thing like years ago with Rusty. I did what he wanted in bed just to make him happy even though it felt icky. I was attracted to his outer appearance until that night. Afterward, every time I looked at him or was around him, he seemed so disturbing, which is why I ended things.

He creeped me out and admitted to screwing around with Felicity, so I guess there were two major reasons why that potential relationship didn't work out.

What I told Taylor the other night was true. No one had ever given me butterflies or flutters in my panties before Hugo. I was really starting to wonder if I were asexual since I had zero interest in men until him. There weren't even any thoughts in my head that were steamy enough for me to get myself off.

But right now? Well, I'm hot just thinking about Hugo's reaction to the video I'm about to record and send to him.

Turning on the camera app on my phone, I press the button to record, then flip the angle so that it's facing me like for a selfie when I place it on the mattress. All that's left is to get on my hands and knees above it.

At first, I just go for it, shoving my hand right down the front of my pajama bottoms and panties before changing my mind. The image is sort of sexy I guess but not the sort of shock and awe I'm going for her.

Sitting back on my heels, I pull my shirt off over my head and then push my bottoms down my legs, kicking them off before resuming the position over the phone.

This time, when I slide my fingers down my belly and touch myself, I can't help but let out a loud moan.

Good thing Harley's room is on the other side of the house.

I push all those motherly thoughts aside and focus on the task at hand – driving Hugo so crazy that he finally has sex with me.

I need this – him – so bad to replace the memories of my last time...

Nope. Not going there.

I close my eyes and spread my knees wider before letting my index and middle finger move lower until they're sliding inside of me. The gasps and moans I make aren't the least bit fake. They're one hundred percent authentic as I finger myself while recording it all on my phone. As my hips start to move faster, I look down and notice that my breasts are making an appearance as they start to sway back and forth.

My entire body shivers as the pleasure builds. But before I let go, I pull my fingers free and grab my vibrator from the nightstand.

Moving down so that my face is on the screen I say through panting breaths, "I wish this was you instead," before I resume the position, turn on the long, thick penis-shaped vibrator, and then start pushing it inside of me.

Hugo

My phone dings while I'm hanging out at the garage with Remy and his brothers for the third night in a row. That's right, I've been shooting the shit with a group of guys when I could've been with a beautiful woman.

I think I've just been...embarrassed. When I was buying the damn toy motorcycle for Harley and replacing all the locks in the house, I thought it was the least I should do for Everly and the little girl.

But then, once they were home, I felt stupid, like I had gone overboard and practically outed myself as one of Harley's potential fathers. It suddenly seemed like I was trying too hard, wanting to make them happy, make Everly happy when I shouldn't care about her at all.

Without even thinking, I pull my phone out in case it's Everly with another emergency and not Abel or Nolan who have been blowing up my phone all day.

It is her.

And when I open up the text chat log, there's a video that's dark and a little blurry until I press play.

"*Oh! Ohhh god!*" Everly's moans come blaring out of the phone's speaker so loud that I nearly drop the damn thing while rushing to turn the volume down.

"What the fuck, man?" Remy looks up from the bike he's working on to ask with a raised blond eyebrow. "What are you watching?"

"Yeah, Hugo, want to share with the class?" Colt says with a bark of laughter as he starts walking over.

"Nope. Just, ah, some, um, porn I forget to close earlier. You know how it is," I lie. "See y'all later," I rush to add as I slip outside into the night.

Shoving the phone into my pocket to make sure it doesn't broadcast Everly's sexy sounds again, I hop on my bike.

I've never rode my Harley so hard or so fast, desperate to get back to my motel room and see the rest of that naughty as hell video.

What was she thinking sending shit like that to a man she's only known for a few days?

Some assholes wouldn't wait two seconds before posting it online, sharing it, her, with their friends or even the entire world.

Me? I might delete it after I watch it tonight just to make sure no one else ever gets a peek at it.

After I watch it a few hundred times, of course.

As soon as I'm finally back in my motel room, I flop down on the bed and start the video over.

It takes several turns of my head to the left and the right as I try to figure out what I'm looking at. And then it becomes abundantly clear.

Everly is kneeling over her phone, undressing before she returns, now just her smooth, bare skin, naked from the waist down, possibly up top too but I can't see that part of her, unfortunately.

I groan aloud when her fingers start moving down her body, heading to the Promised Land.

My own hand moves to the front of my jeans to grab and adjust my growing length before I decide to undo my pants to free my cock.

It's exactly what the woman intended when she sent me the fucking video.

She's tempting me, as if she has no idea that it takes all of my willpower to stay away from her and keep my hands off of her as it is.

Now, after this short little video that I only manage to watch two full times before I come in my fist, I want her so bad it might kill me.

I haven't even cleaned myself up yet when I text her using my clean left hand. It's a slow process, but I manage to tell her: ***Don't move. Stay right there, just like that. I'll let myself in.***

That's right. I'm going over there tonight to lick up every drop of arousal from her pussy. I want to taste the honey that's dripping from her after she got herself off thinking about me.

How do I know she was thinking about me?

Because of those few sweet words she uttered between moans, *"I wish this was you instead,"* right before she shoved a dildo bigger than me when I'm swollen to capacity into her pussy. It was hot as hell to watch, but now I'm fucking jealous of an inanimate object.

It's a good thing I kept a copy of her house key. I'm still glad I didn't waste any time changing all of her locks and checking her windows after her freakshow landlord come busting in the other night, even if it was overkill.

That asshole is lucky I didn't shoot him or beat his ass for pulling that stunt.

Thinking of Everly and Harley there alone, unprotected, it makes me fucking crazy.

Since I can't be there all the time, the least I could do was change the locks, add a deadbolt, and a chain.

Those things wouldn't stop a determined intruder for long, but it would give Everly time to call for help or try to run out the back with Harley.

CHAPTER TWENTY

Everly

I stare at the screen of the phone after I send the video, waiting. For the first few minutes there's nothing.

But then...those little dots appear, then disappear. Appear again, then disappear.

Jeez. Is Hugo writing a freaking novel or something?

Finally, words pop up on the screen.

Don't move. Stay right there, just like that. I'll let myself in.

Holy crap!

He's coming over.

Guess he kept a key, which I'm thankful for at this moment so I won't have to get up and get dressed. Good thing I didn't put the chain up yet tonight either.

My limbs are still recovering from the orgasm I gave myself with the vibrator, although I will have to get up soon to unlock the bedroom door.

God, I feel too good to move at the moment, though.

I've tried getting myself off with the device several times before, but it never worked. I couldn't ever get images of the last time I had sex out of my head to think about something that turned me on. I would always hear Rusty's incessant commentary in my ear.

Until Hugo came along.

Thinking about him barging into my bedroom, ripping his clothes off, and then jumping on top of me, well, I was slick and coming in no time at all.

I just hope I'm tight enough for him.

Rusty complained that since I wasn't a virgin, I didn't feel as good for him the one time we had sex. With comments like that, we never repeated the act.

Guys don't seem to have that problem with Felicity, though, and she's been with a ton of men.

It's possible I have some deformity down there that I don't know about since I've never compared that particular body part with any other woman.

Hugo would've mentioned if something was off when he fingered me and licked me, right?

At the sound of the back door softly opening and closing, I go so still I don't even breath, listening, waiting.

How in the world did he get here so fast? He must have broken a few traffic laws to drive from the motel to the house in less than five minutes. And figured out the combination for the lock on the gate.

I slide off the side of the bed and walk on wobbling legs to the door, flipping the lock just before the doorknob turns.

Hugo slips inside my room then closes the door. My lower body clenches in expectation at the sound of him turning the lock into place.

"Jesus fucking Christ," he whispers as his eyes sweep up and down my body several times. Even in the heat of the moment he hasn't forgotten that Harley is sleeping down the hall and that we have to keep it down. That small thing makes him even hotter, if that's possible. He may wear the same leather and jeans every day, but the clothes don't make the man. I'm pretty sure this man could look sexy and imposing even in a speedo.

"Hey," I reply as I stand before him, unsure what else to say. I push a lock of my long hair behind my ear while I wait for him to make a move.

"I thought I told you not to move," his deep voice rumbles darkly.

"I, ah, I had to unlock the door." I point at the fixture behind him in explanation.

"Get back on the bed. I want you in the same position – on your hands and knees."

"Oh. Okay," I agree as I take a step backward before turning around to climb up on the foot of the bed. I crawl to the middle and then wait as instructed. Guess we're going to have sex doggy style. I've never done that before. There's a long list of things I've never done with a man. In fact, it would be easier to make a list of what I have done – sex missionary with all three men, along with one creepy fantasy played out. It was always over too fast for me to feel much. I don't think that will be an issue with a man like Hugo.

I wait and listen, but still haven't heard him move. When I glance behind me, he's still standing in the exact same spot, staring at me, making me self-conscious.

"Changed my mind," he says as he finally moves closer until he's next to the bed. Grabbing one of my pillows, he tosses it in front of me. "Face down so nothing but your ass is in the air."

"S-sure," I agree, lowering the side of my face until my cheek is resting on the pillow as I watch him. I expect him to start getting undressed, but he doesn't, he just walks around to the foot of the bed so that I can't see him without lifting my head. I don't do that because not looking at him is better in this embarrassing position.

The mattress behind me dips as I assume Hugo climbs up.

All at the same time and without warning, both of his hands are grabbing almost painful fistfuls of my ass cheeks and his flattened tongue is licking me from clit to asshole, making me gasp and shiver.

"Mmm," he groans. "I missed the taste of your sweet pussy."

His tongue takes the opposite path this time, making me tremble and moan his name. "Hugo...please. I need..."

"What do you need?" he asks as the tip of his tongue batters my clit, making speaking impossible. "Ev?"

It takes several tries before I manage to tell him, "You! Inside of me!"

I know he had to have heard me, but his tongue just continues its savage attack on that bundle of nerves until my eyes close on a moan and my entire body shakes with pleasure.

I bite down on the pillow to keep from screaming through the incredible tremors.

Hugo's lips and tongue move over me, kissing me, sucking me between my legs, lapping up every drop of my arousal.

My body is tingling, feeling amazing, but still I need more. I need his body moving inside of mine. So, I decide to use words that leave no room for interpretation. "Fuck me, Hugo!"

"No," is his quiet, one-word response between his naughty kisses.

"W-what?" I ask. When he doesn't answer, I say, "Why won't you just...fuck me?"

There's a moment of silence, followed by a gruff, "Because I don't deserve the honor of sliding my cock into the hot, wet, heaven between your legs."

What the heck does that mean?

"But your...tongue is-is okay between my legs?" I ask between pants.

"Oh yeah," he says, talking to me between long, urgent, licks up to my asshole again like he's trying to eat a dripping ice cream cone in the middle of July. "I'll tongue this pretty pussy anytime you need me to. You're so swollen and needy from fucking yourself. I can't get enough."

"Hugo!" I shout as that talented tongue of his starts flicking over my sensitive flesh again until I'm racing toward that blissful cliff again.

"That's right, blondie, rub your cunt all over my face, whatever it takes to get off. If you need a thick finger to get there, I've got plenty of those too."

"Yes! Now!" I exclaim, needing just a little something more...him filling the emptiness inside of me.

Hugo eases one thick digit into my throbbing pussy, and I explode around it.

I can't see or hear or think. I'm just spiraling into oblivion until I slump into the darkness.

CHAPTER TWENTY-ONE

Hugo

W hen Everly's ass falls sideways down to the mattress, I figure she must have had enough.

I lift the collar of my t-shirt to dry my mouth as I lean up to look at her face. Her eyes are shut, lips still parted in an O...and she's sound asleep.

Well, that's one way to keep me from pulling my dick out to feel her tight, wet heat squeezing around it.

I was close to caving when she asked me to fuck her. I know the f-word isn't a term she uses often, if ever. She was hurting, and I wanted to make it better by giving her anything she wanted even if I didn't have a condom and doubt that she does either...

A rattling noise from the front of the house makes me freeze for a second before I pull the bedding up to cover Everly, then ease quietly off the bed.

It's probably Harley going to the bathroom or getting some water.

Hopefully she didn't hear Everly. I doubt it since the woman bit into the pillow to muffle her moans. I've never had a woman do that before, and it was sexy as hell.

I hesitate between staying in the bedroom so that Harley won't see me here this late at night and going to check to see what the sound I heard was.

When I hear it again, I say screw it. Unlocking the bedroom door, I slip out quietly and start walking to the front of the house. The noise isn't Harley. The house is empty, but the sound is someone outside jiggling the shit out of the doorknob.

And if I had a million dollars, I would bet it all that it's Everly's pain in the ass landlord again.

Suddenly, something Ev said when we were having dinner comes back to me.

Didn't she say that she dated the landlord years ago?

Is the asshole still hung up on her? Is that why he's here so late at night? He thinks he has a chance with her?

She would've told me if she was still hooking up with him, wouldn't she?

Fuck yes. Ev is nothing but one-hundred percent honest about everything.

She told me they dated right after she moved back home, five years ago.

He had to have been the last man she fucked.

I peek out one of the front windows and see the curly-haired bastard take several steps back with his hands on his hips. His hair is messy, and he looks ticked off that he couldn't bust in and stop me from eating Ev's pussy again.

Hold on.

It can't be a coincidence that he would show up right now, in the middle of the night after Everly and I fooled around *and* the other day when she was in the middle of giving me head.

How would he possibly know that we were hooking up at the exact right time?

There's only one fucking way.

And if I'm right, that son of a bitch is a dead man.

Everly

"Ev, WAKE UP."

"Mmm," I murmur and smile at the sound of Hugo's grumbly voice, his lips next to my ear, kissing me there. "Don't stop."

"Sorry, blondie, but you need to wake up. Right now."

This time his voice is harder, losing all softness, making my eyes finally blink open. I'm curled up naked on the bed with the comforter laid over me while he stands next to it.

"We need to leave," Hugo says.

"Huh?" I sit up and brush my sweaty hair out of my face, trying to clear the fuzziness out of my head. He thinks we need to...leave?

"Can you pack a bag and then wake up Harley?"

"What? No. I can't wake her up!"

"Please, Ev," Hugo says, his eyes serious and pleading.

"Tell me why?"

"I can't right now. I will, though. Later. Just...can you trust me?"

I stare at him, waiting to see if he's going to crack a smile and tell me he's kidding. But he doesn't. Not that he's the type to pull some type of silly prank. And even though I haven't known him long, I do trust him.

"Um, okay. Fine. I need to get dressed. Can you..." Suddenly I'm feeling self-conscious again.

"I'll wait in the living room," he says. "Just hurry. My motel room is shit. Is there somewhere else you two can stay tonight?"

"Ah, yeah. I guess I could call Taylor..."

"Good. Call her. Tell her we're on the way."

"Okay," I agree with a nod, wondering if this is a dream. It seems too strange to be actually happening.

Hugo stops in the doorway with his phone in his hand. "One other thing. Could you, ah, give me Remy's number?" That has me leaning away from the dream idea since there is no reason I would bring up my cousin in one.

"You want...my cousin's phone number?"

"Yes," Hugo grits out between clenched teeth.

He must have a good reason, so I press a hand to my forehead to try and remember the seven digits without finding my phone. When I finally do, I rattle off the numbers that Hugo quickly punches into his phone. "Thanks," he says as he walks out.

As soon as he's gone, the first thing I do is put on my pajama pants and tank top again, then call Taylor, hoping she won't hate me for waking her up so late at night and asking to barge in on her family, especially since I don't even know why.

The line rings so many times that I assume it's going to go to voicemail. But then, her groggy voice says, "Everly? Everything okay?"

"Hey, I need a favor, but I'm not sure why."

"Anything," she says.

"Can I bring Harley over and both of us stay with you tonight?"

"Sure. Did something happen?"

"Ah, Hugo came over and he just woke me with instructions. He says he can't explain right now, that I just need to hurry up and throw things in a bag and wake up Harley."

"Jeez. That's not cryptic at all," she replies, sounding more awake.

"I'm sorry."

"No, it's no problem. The guest room is ready. I'll make up the futon bed in the playroom for Harley and put on a pot of coffee for us."

"Great, thank you so much," I tell her.

When I hang up, I turn to my dresser and catch my reflection in the mirror above it. My hair is a tangled mess, my cheeks are still flushed from earlier, and my eyes look bright and...happy? Everything feels sort of odd, unreal again. But then Hugo's knuckles rap on the door, followed by a quiet, "You about ready?"

"Just about," I call back.

I throw some clothes in an oversized purse from my closet, grab a clean outfit for Harley from the laundry room, and then it's time to wake her up and hope she doesn't have a screaming tantrum.

CHAPTER TWENTY-TWO

Hugo

"We'll head that way now," Remy says through the phone just before Everly comes out of the laundry room with her big bag on her shoulder.

"I appreciate it. See ya." I end the call without waiting for his response and follow Everly to Harley's bedroom door.

"I hate to wake her up," Everly says softly.

"I know, but we need to go."

"Fine," she says with a heavy sigh.

When she starts forward, I grab her arm. "Let me just carry her. She may not even wake up on the ride over."

"Okay," Everly agrees with a nod.

Going over to the twin bed, I slide my arms underneath the covers and her small, sleeping body and then lift her against my chest, blankets and all. She's so light, it feels as if I'm just carrying an armful of laundry. It makes me wonder just how tiny she would've been when she was just a baby.

I turn toward Everly and open my mouth to ask before I think better of it. "Grab her pillow, will you?"

"S-sure," Everly replies.

I start making my way through the house, careful to avoid banging Harley's head or feet on the walls, then wait for Everly to unlock and open the front door and car door. I get the sleeping angel in no problem, then shut the door as quietly as possible.

"I'll follow you to Taylor's on my bike."

"Okay," Everly thankfully agrees since I want to make sure they get there okay and then help her carry Harley inside before I go take care of some business.

THE FULTON BROTHERS make good on their promise.

Despite the fact that it's almost one o'clock in the morning, they're all at the address Remy gave me by the time I got Ev and Harley settled in and safe at Taylor's. The two-story, sprawling estate with columns out front is a good half a mile from any other homes, which is perfect considering my plan.

The guys are all smoking cigarettes by their bikes in the circular driveway when my headlight shines on them. I pull up on the far side and kill the engine on my own Harley. Why the hell are all four of them out here?

It suddenly occurs to me that with the five of us, we would have enough people to start a new Savage Kings MC chapter.

Not that I'm planning on moving up here or anything like that. And I have no idea if the Fulton Four are Kings' material or if they would even be interested in forming a club.

Setting aside those crazy ass ideas to think about some other time, I ask them, "Where is he? Why isn't anyone inside with him?" while climbing off my bike.

Remy steps forward, the oldest brother the obvious leader of the group. "Well..." he drawls. "If we told you you're soon to be sleeping with the fishes, how angry would you be?"

Jesus Christ. They killed him? No wonder they're all out here smoking.

"Pretty fuckin pissed," I huff. "I wanted to do the honors," I remark when we're face-to-face. "I told you to subdue him, make sure he doesn't leave until I got here."

"I know," Remy says. Tossing down his cigarette he stomps it out on the paved driveway a little harder than is necessary. "I remember. But the whole plan went to shit when we saw his bedroom."

"What was in his bedroom?" I ask. When Remy looks away, I glance over at the other brothers, all of which are avoiding eye contact. "That can't be good."

"It's..." RJ blows out a puff of smoke before continuing, "Unimaginable psycho shit."

"You don't want to see it, Hugo," Barrett adds, which only makes me more curious. Now, I have to know, so I start marching toward the front of the house.

"Do what you want," Remy calls out as he and the others follow me to the door. "Just remember we warned you."

"Have you all considered how to make him 'swim with the fishes' without it coming back on any of us?"

"Oh, yeah," Colt speaks up. "His forehead is crushed in, so we'll rig up his car and run him off the bridge."

"Then, ah, I've got to do some quick home renovations," Remy mutters.

"You're the one who slammed his head through a wall?" When we're on the porch, I see the head-sized dent in the steel door. "It was the door, huh? You can fix it without it smelling like fresh paint and shit? Oh, and don't forget to gather up all of those cigarette butts with your DNA all over them."

"You're actually handling this mess better than we expected," Remy says rather than answering my question.

"Yeah, we thought you might get all hysterical and shit," Barrett adds.

"You expected me to get hysterical because y'all didn't wait for me?" I ask over my shoulder as I head inside and step over the motionless body to find the bedroom.

"Ah, no," Remy replies. "We thought you would freak out about the dead man you just stepped over like he was a pile of dog shit you didn't want to get on your boots."

"Not my first dead body. Probably won't be the last," I mutter. "I wish I could've done the deed myself, but the result is what's important, making sure that fucker never goes near Everly or Harley again."

"Our thoughts exactly," RJ agrees. "Ah, I'll wait here."

"Me too," Colt and Barrett say at the same time.

That has my feet coming to a sudden stop. "It must be bad if they prefer to wait with the dead body than go back in the bedroom."

"It is," Remy agrees, the last man standing. Sighing, he waves a hand toward the staircase and says, "Let's get it over with."

"Yeah," I agree, finally taking those steps to the second floor. He directs me to the first bedroom on the left.

When he flips on the overhead light, I realize he was right.

I should've listened to the brothers and never gone into that goddamn bedroom.

CHAPTER TWENTY-THREE

Everly

"So, he just woke you up and said pack your shit, let's go?" Taylor asks when she slides a steaming mug of coffee in front of me and sits down on the other side of the kitchen table with a cup of her own.

"Pretty much. He said he couldn't tell me right then why but would later. Now here we are. Thankfully, Harley didn't wake up." I blow on my coffee, then take a sip while meeting Taylor's stare from across the table. "What?"

"Aren't you going to tell me why Hugo was at your house while you were sleeping?"

"Oh. That." I try to keep a straight face but fail when the corners of my lips curl up.

"I want all of the details!" she whispers loudly.

I push my coffee away to cover my heating face with both hands. "It's so embarrassing."

"Come on, Ev. Just tell me."

"Fine," I mutter when I drop my hands. "I sent Hugo a video earlier tonight."

"A video?" she repeats.

"Uh-huh."

"A naughty video?"

"Yes."

"Ooh. Most girls just send dirty photos. You made an entire video?"

"It was short," I remark. "He hadn't sent a message all day and didn't come by. I wanted to get his attention and have the upper hand for once."

"It obviously worked. What did you send him?"

"I, ah, I was doing myself while giving him a very close up shot of it all. I may have mentioned that I would rather it was him."

"Damn. No wonder he came running over."

I laugh at that comment. "He had to have broken some land speed records to get there as fast as he did."

"And then? Did you finally have s-e-x?" Taylor spells the word even though all the little ones are sound asleep.

"No," I admit with a sigh of disappointment.

"No? Are you joking?"

I shake my head. "We did stuff. He did incredible things to me but got nothing in return. Again.

"Still nothing on his side? Is he deformed or something down there? Have a tiny, pencil prick?"

"No, definitely not any problems with him down there. I've felt and seen it. He's...perfect in every way, length and width."

"So, then what is the hold up? What is wrong with that man?"

"That's what I keep asking myself."

"A man who enjoys getting a woman off more than himself? Those are hard to find. I mean, I lucked up, but you haven't dated or had sex in years. Girl, do whatever it takes to keep him even if you have to put a ring on it."

I smile at that statement before admitting to her, "We were so close the other night, right before Rusty came by. I was...I was on my knees and everything."

"Jeez. I bet Hugo was pissed that you two got interrupted before he finished his blowie!"

"Oh yeah, he was livid. I heard him yelling at Rusty. The jerk should be glad I intervened before Hugo threw a punch at him."

"He was that upset, huh?"

"He was. Not just that we had to stop, but also because Rusty used his key to let himself in before Hugo could get to the door! That really ticked him off."

"No kidding. I get that he owns the place, but that's really messed up that he would barge right on in."

"I know. It was, but I had called Rusty about the roof leaking and left him a message, so I guess it was sort of my fault. Still, even if Rusty gets upset about Hugo changing the locks and adding more, I don't care. He's creepy."

"Yes, he is," Taylor agrees. "I mean, sure Rusty is classically handsome on the outside. But after you dated him and he slept with Felicity behind your back, I only saw him as a big, stinky pile of garbage."

"Same."

"So, once he was gone, did you finish Hugo off?"

"Nope. He just made an excuse and left!"

"He left and then came back to change your locks for you?"

"Yes. By Friday afternoon he had changed the locks and bought and put together a pink Harley for Harley."

"Really? Wow. That man is not like any other."

"No, he's not," I agree. "He confuses me like crazy, and yet I keep begging for more. Literally."

"There's no shame in that, Ev. Enjoy yourself until you figure him out."

"I think his hang-ups with sex are maybe like emotional or mental. There's something holding him back, I'm just not sure what.

163

And while I want to keep enjoying myself, I have a feeling it's only a matter of time before he leaves town, never to be seen or heard from again."

"You've known from the start that he was just passing through, though," Taylor points out. "You were fine with him being a no-strings attached hookup then. What changed?"

I drum my fingers on the counters and think about how to answer her question. "He's really good with Harley."

"Yeah?"

"Yeah. I didn't expect him to be. If anything, I thought finding out I was raising her would send him running. Instead, he talks to her like...like she's an adult instead of a child. It's sweet, and she appreciates being taken so seriously by him. He said he doesn't have much experience around kids"

"Huh."

"What does that huh mean?" I ask with my brow raised.

"Nothing. I was just thinking maybe it's possible that he's getting to the age where he wants to settle down. Find a place to park his bike for more than a few nights, if you know what I mean."

"That's the thing, though! He won't park his bike in me no matter what I do!"

"Guys are strange. If they sleep with you fast, then they weren't looking for anything serious. But if they wait...sometimes I think it's because they want more than a hookup."

"You really think Hugo would give up the MC in South Carolina to stay here? There's no way..."

"Don't give up on him just yet. It sounds like he cares about you and wants to be with you. Why else would he rush you over here in the middle of the night?"

"That's true."

"He wants you, Ev. It's only a matter of time before he gives in."

"I hope you're right. Now if I only knew where the heck he is and what in the world he's doing tonight..."

Hugo

WELL, I wanted a surefire way to push Everly away for good.

When she finds out what happened tonight, she isn't going to want anything to do with me. Especially not as a father-figure for Harley.

Is that why I put all of this in motion in the first place? Because I was looking for an out?

I honestly don't fucking know.

One thing is certain, I don't have any regrets about the man's death. Not because I don't consider it on my hands, because I do. It's all on me. I called Remy. I'm the one who got that murderous ball rolling. I mean, I had a suspicion when I called the boys, but I didn't really think...I couldn't have imagined...

Here's hoping the brothers can keep their mouths closed.

I think they will.

None of us will ever want to talk or even think about tonight again.

That fucking dude was one sick son of a bitch.

There's no way to know if he ever acted on his fetishes other than the videos we found. If there are more victims, then, well, they're all safer without him around.

So, if I'm good with the stain on my soul, why am I still sitting on my bike refusing to go knock on Taylor's door or text Everly to let her know I'm back?

It's not because of the late hour. I have no doubt that both women are still awake, wondering what the hell is going on.

I think the real reason I'm stalling is because I'm not ready to tell Everly the truth and let her go just yet.

It's so stupid of me to start falling for the one woman I can't ever be with.

Eventually, she'll find out about Felicity, whether or not I'm Harley's father. And if there's one thing I've learned about the sweet, outgoing woman, it's that she doesn't want anything to do with any of her sister's sloppy seconds.

While I was hanging out at the shop the other night with the guys, Remy mentioned that Everly has always been in Felicity's shadow when it comes to men. Even though Ev is way more beautiful, guys want to fuck the wild, stripper, not the nice little schoolteacher.

No, Everly is the type of woman you settle down with and marry. Felicity is the girl who loves money more than anything else. It's why she has no problem being degraded and used for a few nights before moving on to someone with deeper pockets.

Young guys, especially teenagers, were all going to shoot their shot with Felicity in high school, not her sweet, younger sister, who is so gorgeous you know the odds of ever being able to touch her are slim to none. Why waste time on a woman who says *maybe* when you can have the woman who is a sure thing?

I get it.

Five years ago, Abel and I both couldn't get enough of the freaky stripper who let us do anything we wanted to her as long as the cash kept flowing.

She wasn't a straight prostitute. No, she convinced us to buy her nice shit in expensive stores and thanked us with blowjobs in the changing room.

The three of us knew the score at the time, and it worked for us. At least for a few weeks.

Then Nolan got arrested, and Abel and I were up and moving again to be closer to the facility where our friend did his time so we could visit as often as possible.

That was when Abel and I first moved in together, and when I began to realize he might be bisexual. He was never obvious about it.

At least not until more recently when I started to notice that he couldn't finish unless my dick was getting sucked at the same time or he was getting sucked off while I took a woman from behind. He probably thought I wouldn't notice his quick glances at my dick. Guess the part of me that loves being an exhibitionist just didn't care.

For some reason, the idea of fucking Everly in front of someone else pops into my head, making me hard and furious all at the same time.

I don't want anyone to see her or us together. And I sure as shit wouldn't share her with a soul, not even my best friend.

She's a good girl who would never have sex outside of the bedroom, mostly because a minor lives in the house, but also because she's a rule follower and shy when it comes to screwing.

At least I thought she was before I got that video earlier tonight. That was something I never would've thought Everly would do. Damn, if she didn't just do it, but she was also sexy as hell, not the last bit reserved like the few times we've fooled around before.

The thought *I can't wait to see what she'll do next* pops into my head before I realize that I won't ever find out.

Not after I go into the house and tell her what happened tonight. She's going to ask, and this is one thing I can't lie to her about. She needs to know even if it means hating me and never wanting to see me again.

Fuck if that doesn't make my dick settle down.

I'm going to miss Everly. Not just her sexy side, but the sweet, motherly one too, more than I realized.

CHAPTER TWENTY-FOUR

Everly

"Did you hear that?" I ask Taylor as we both finish up our second cup of coffee. It probably wasn't a good idea, because instead of being sleepy, now I'm wired.

"Yeah, it sounded like a soft knock at the door," she agrees as we both start heading for the front of the house.

"It's probably Hugo not wanting to wake everyone up."

Taylor looks out the peephole and says, "Yep, it's him. I'll, ah, leave you two alone. Holler if you need me?"

"Thanks," I tell her and then start turning the locks. "You're back," I say to him when I finally get the door opened.

Hugo's shoulders are more slumped than usual under his leather cut, like the weight of the world is on his shoulders.

"Everything okay?"

"Can you come outside so we can talk?" he asks.

Oh hell no. If I go outside with him, then he'll say a few words and leave like Friday.

"No, but we can go into the guest bedroom and talk," I tell him as I grab his hand and pull him inside. I lock up, then drag him through the living room and kitchen to the end of the hallway.

Once we're inside the bedroom, I shut the door and then go sit on the foot of the bed, my arms crossed over my chest. "Are you going to *finally* tell me what's going on now?" I ask.

"I couldn't tell you before, because, well, I didn't want to give him a warning that I was on to him."

I replay that sentence over and over in my head trying to make it make sense. It doesn't. "Give *who* a warning, Hugo?"

"Rusty."

I stagger to my feet, confused beyond belief now. "Rusty? What does my landlord have to do with anything?"

"Sit back down, Everly."

"Why?"

"Could you please just stop asking questions and let me talk?"

"Sure, if you're actually going to talk to me using less vague statements."

"I will," he says softly with a heavy sigh as he leans his head against the closed door and closes his eyes. For the first time, I notice that not only does he seem frustrated, but he also looks exhausted. Where has he been for the past few hours after he dropped me and Harley off?

I hold back the rest of my questions, trying to wait patiently for Hugo to speak as I retake my seat on the foot of the bed.

"You mentioned it in passing before, and Remy confirmed that you and Rusty used to be...together."

"Wow," I mutter since that was the last thing I expected him to say. When he just keeps standing there, staring at me, I assume he wants me to provide more information. "Yes, we dated a long time ago. It was never serious or anything."

"You slept with him."

170

"That's—" I start to say it's none of his business, but Hugo holds up his palm to stop me. "I already know you did. Do you want me to tell you how I know that?"

I frown and swallow around a sudden knot in my throat and nod my head yes. Taylor is the only person I ever told. She may have mentioned it to Kyle, but I doubt it. So how does Hugo know? "Has Rusty been running his mouth?" I can't help but ask Hugo.

"No. He recorded you. Together. I saw the video tonight."

"He what?" I whisper.

"There were cameras in his bedroom. He recorded the whole thing, at least one of the times you were there."

"There was only one time. Ever."

"At his place?"

"Yes," I reply softly as I think back to that strange night four or so years ago, trying to remember everything that was captured on video to be watched over and over. The parts of me he recorded without my permission or knowledge....

"Was it just role playing or not, Ev? I have to know the truth even if I would rather rip my ears off than hear about it."

Oh. Right.

I nod my head. "Just role playing."

"You can tell me the truth."

I clear my throat, trying to find my voice to answer without looking away in embarrassment. "I know I could, Hugo. But that is the truth. He...he played a DVD and told me it would be hot if I reenacted it. He wasn't my first, though."

Hugo shuts his eyes again and takes a deep breath, his chest moving up and down slowly. "At least there's that."

"The woman on the video was pretending it was her first time too," I rush to explain. "At least that's what he assured me at the time. Still, it was creepy, and I didn't like it."

Hugo looks up at me again. "That's why you didn't sleep with him again?"

"Mostly."

"Mostly?"

"He told me that night that my sister was a better actress during sex, much more vocal and believable. He wanted me to be more like her the next time."

"Him and Felicity?"

"Yes. Before we..." I shake my head. "Rusty tried to tell me that it was before we started dating, but Felicity admitted it was a few days before the night I was with him. She was getting close to her delivery date, so she was big and pregnant and was just 'trying to induce labor' and Rusty offered to help her. He tried to use the same excuse when he begged me to forgive him and give him another chance. I refused."

"I'm guessing he didn't give up easily?" Hugo asks.

"Ah, no. He was persistent. He kept calling me and coming by the house. Then Harley was born, and I was too busy to fool with him bothering me."

"Everly, I hate to tell you this, but the guy was obsessed with you. He still had your video, like, in his DVD player."

"Huh?"

"In his bed, he even had this-this fucking mannequin with blonde hair dressed in something you would wear. There were holes cut out so he could...well, you know."

"That's..." I can't even figure out what to say to that since it sounds so freaking weird.

"He installed cameras in your house too, Ev. Every day, every night, he was watching you in this goddamn command center in his room."

I'm certain I must have misheard Hugo. "There are cameras in *my* house?"

"Yes. In your bedroom, the living room, and the, ah, bathroom."

"Oh my god," I whisper as I slap my trembling hand over my gapping mouth. God, that's so sick and disgusting knowing he was watching me without me knowing it, seeing everything I did in bed, in the shower, ew, even on the toilet. That's so disgusting I just want to throw up.

"I'm so sorry, Ev. I wish I had found them sooner."

Now, finally, it all makes sense, why Hugo woke me up and rushed us out of the house.

"You saw them tonight? The, um, the cameras? That's why you wanted us to leave? Because you didn't want to give him a warning....that's what you said."

So, I guess that also answers the question of where Hugo's been.

I almost feel sorry for the beatdown he must have given to Rusty, but no, I don't. I thought he was creepy; I just had no idea he was so freaking sick.

"Did you know he came by the house tonight?" Hugo asks me, and I shake my head no. "He was angry when his key didn't work. I thought it was strange how he showed up when we were fooling around the first time in your room, then tonight. It couldn't have been a coincidence. It had nothing to do with the flooding. Hell, he may have known before you called and did nothing about it!" Hugo runs his fingers through his hair as his face contorts in anger. "Once I saw the cameras in the air vents and knew for sure, that was it. I couldn't let him watch you another second."

"What did you do to him?" I ask, wanting to know. Needing to know. I'm not usually one to condone violence, but this time I'll easily make an exception. If I wasn't so embarrassed, I would want to confront him and hit him myself.

Still talking while looking at the floor and not me, Hugo says, "He had an entire wall, floor to ceiling of violent porn on DVDs, and he was clearly obsessed with you, Ev. It was only a matter of time before he acted on that shit."

"Hugo? What did you do? You can tell me..."

"There were videos of girls Harley's age too. Videos of Harley in the bath... That's why he couldn't live to see another day."

Oh my god! That's so disturbing that there are no words. He deserves to spend the rest of his life behind bars. That's what Hugo is trying to say. Hopefully. "Rusty will definitely be going to prison for the rest of his life. That's what you mean, right?"

"Rusty won't be seeing his day in court. He died in a car accident tonight, ran right off the bridge and died instantly before the car sank into the sound." Hugo tells me Rusty's dead like it's a well-rehearsed line of a script.

Holy shit. Rusty's dead?

I should feel sad or guilty or something, but I don't. All I feel is... relieved, which probably makes me a horrible person. But after what Hugo just told me, if even half of it is true, well, I would never have felt safe again.

He took a man's life for me.

And while what he did, taking a life, is wrong on so many levels, and I could never hurt anyone myself, I'm glad that Hugo did what he had to do to protect me, to protect Harley from that sick bastard.

Hearing that Rusty is dead, my first concern is not for him or his loved ones. I don't think he even had any. No, I'm mostly just worried about what this means for the house I was renting from him, if I'm going to have to up and move Harley, who hates even the smallest changes in her life because she's been hurt so badly by her mother.

"How did you...." I trail off and then remember him asking for Remy's number before he left. "My cousins helped you, didn't they?"

"I ended that piece of shit, Ev. Me. Not them. Don't blame your family for any of this."

"If Remy, Colt, Barrett, and RJ found out even half of the things you told me about just now, they wouldn't have thought twice about hurting him."

"Those guys are serious about protecting their family. It's not a bad thing."

"They're involved, Hugo. I know that, and I wish I could understand how you could do that or why, but I can't."

"I didn't expect you to," he grumbles. "I'll go. I just thought you should know. The cameras in the house are gone now."

174

When he turns around and reaches for the doorknob, it hits me that he's actually leaving. How could he possibly leave after dropping that enormous, elephant-sized bomb on me?

"Hugo, wait!" I say as I scramble off the bed to grab his arm and tug on it, urging him to turn around.

Staring down on me as I grip his bare arm, he says, "I'll understand if you need to go to the police. They won't find me. The Kings will make sure of that. Just don't drag your cousins into it."

"What?" I ask in confusion before I realize that he's giving me his permission to turn him in for murder. Jesus. "No, Hugo. I'm not going to turn you in or my cousins. God, my uncle is the deputy sheriff! If he finds out about...well, he'll probably have Rusty cremated before the sun comes up to hide the evidence!"

Hugo's eyes widen just a little in surprise before he says, "Remy said the exact same thing."

"I'm used to the whole macho, tough guy, badass act. I grew up with six older male cousins who would fight first and ask questions later when we were just kids. If anything, their tempers have gotten worse, not better, when it comes to family."

"I'm glad you're not angry at them," Hugo says.

"I'm not angry at you either."

"You're not? Are you kidding me right now?"

I take a step forward to press my forehead to his chest, loving how strong he feels, letting his masculine sweat and leather smell fill my nose and listen to his heart thumping away. "That night with Rusty, it may have been consensual, and I'm glad I wasn't *actually* a virgin like he made me pretend, but it still scarred me. He's the real reason I haven't gone out with anyone or slept with anyone. I was afraid I would trust a man again and have them turn out to be something completely different. Something dark. I didn't want to go through that sort of betrayal again."

"Ev..." Hugo starts, but I lift my head and go up on my toes to cover his mouth with mine. Our lips touch and separate three soft times before I tell him, "Shut up and kiss me, Hugo."

His hands grip my shoulders, trying to hold me back. "How the hell could you still want me after what I just told you?"

"How could I not want you?"

"You should hate me or at least be scared of me now," he says.

"I think I hated Rusty for getting in my head and never leaving. But you, I can't hate you, Hugo. Don't you get it yet? I need you to help me forget my last time and replace it with something good."

His grip loosens on my arms, hands moving to grab the back of my neck, holding my lips to his before his tongue swipes into my parted lips. The move makes my knees weak and my panties wet.

"We shouldn't," he has the audacity to say a moment later against my lips.

I grab the hem of my pajama top and yank it over my head, then brace a palm on his hard chest for balance when I shove my bottoms and panties down my legs and step out of them.

Now I'm completely naked, standing before the man who confuses me so much that I honestly don't know if he'll still walk out the door or not. If he does, well, I certainly won't chase him or beg him to be with me. One more rejection from him and I'm done for good.

I stand there looking up at his face with both of my palms splayed on his t-shirt covered chest in the opening of his leather cut, waiting. His eyes look darker than ever before when he leans his back against the door to glance down the length of my figure. I drop my hands from him, but his big ones move down from my neck to my arms, my sides, then tightly grasp my hips.

"I should've told you everything about tonight by text message instead of in-person," is what the infuriating man finally says when his gaze locks with mine again.

My cheeks blaze hot with embarrassment and resentment. I slap my palms angrily against his chest. The move forces me back instead of him since he's already plastered to the damn door. "No one is forcing you to be here, asshole!"

Hugo groans, and quicker than I can blink, he grabs my wrists to yank me forward to the front of his body at the same time. I gasp when my soft curves crash into his hard body. "You're so fucking sexy when you're angry." That's what it sounds like he says before his tongue is suddenly invading my mouth with the kind of domination and force that reminds me of when he used the body part between my legs earlier tonight.

CHAPTER TWENTY-FIVE

Hugo

Everly doesn't hate me and isn't afraid of me after I told her I killed a man.

How is that possible?

I may have exaggerated a little, trying to make her cousins look as innocent as possible, but even knowing everything, she's naked for the second time tonight and she's kissing me.

Did I even kiss her mouth earlier? When we were in her bedroom?

Fuck. I don't think I did. I couldn't pull my mouth from her pussy long enough to capture her lips.

Now, I have to pull away for a different reason.

"Ev, we can't. I don't have a condom."

"I'm on the pill."

Four simple words that could have life changing consequences.

She wants me to fuck her bareback.

179

This woman trusts me to not give her an STD.

She wants me to trust her when she tells me she's on birth control and won't get knocked up with my kid.

There are so many reasons why I should stop right now and not let this go any further.

But I no longer just want this beautiful woman. I need to be with her, to have her in a way that makes her mine and no one else's, at least for a little while longer.

So, when she undoes the front of my jeans with shaking hands, I don't stop her. Instead, I shove the denim down my legs. Not wanting to let her go long enough to even get my clothes off, I grab Everly's ass cheeks and lift her before I lower us both to the floor, sitting down and keeping my back against the door.

I didn't consider that having her straddling my lap while both of us are naked where it counts would feel too good to worry about silly shit like my jeans around my ankles or the boots still on my feet.

Our bodies just naturally come together and fit perfectly. There are no cares or concerns about anything else for the moment. All I know is that nothing has ever felt as good as being buried inside of Everly's body, swallowing her soft whimpers with my lips as I fill her, her fingers tangled in my hair while mine dig into her gorgeous ass as I move her up and down on my cock.

Isn't that why I've refused to give in and be with her before now? Because I fucking knew that once I had her, I would never be able to get enough of her.

"Yes! *Ohmygodyes!*" Everly cries out in a desperate jumble when her mouth finally breaks free from mine as her pussy pulses around my cock, soaking me in her hot, thick release.

I pump my hips up into her at the same time her body slams down on me, both of us moving faster and faster, our hands gripping each other so tightly we may leave bruises. I just can't get close enough no matter what I do, wanting Everly inside of me while I'm inside of her.

The thought doesn't make a damn bit of sense in my head, but my chest understands. It cracks wide open down the middle, letting her in along with a flood of emotions I've never experienced before. It feels like I'm drowning in them, in her.

Everly sighs as she rests her head on my shoulder and her lower body begins to relax. I thrust up into her hard, making her gasp when I remind her that we're not finished yet.

Leaning forward I cover her nipple with my mouth, sucking on it hard, flicking my tongue over it before letting it go with a pop.

"We're not done yet, blondie," I warn her as I lower her back to the carpeted floor, putting more of my weight on her. "You're mine now, baby. You'll come on my cock at least one more time before I'm finished fucking you."

"Hugo," Everly whispers, her eyes closing as she works her hips up and down on me. "Don't...ever...stop."

While I wish I could stay right here in this room inside of her forever, all good things must come to an end, including our first time.

So when Everly throws her head back just as her body trembles with another release, I lean down and cover her smooth neck with my mouth, muffling my groans as I empty myself inside of her.

Everly

"What's with you and doors?" I ask from underneath Hugo once all of my five senses eventually return to me, along with oxygen in my lungs. He's still above me, propped up on his elbows.

"Doors?" he repeats while staring at the strand of my hair he's currently coiling tightly around his finger.

"Yeah, the wooden things that have been there when you first kissed me, felt me up, went down on me, and now..."

"Oh," he mutters.

181

"Well? Odd coincidence, right?" I ask with a smile on my face that may be permanent after those two earth-shattering orgasms.

"Not really," Hugo replies. "Every time we're together I know I should walk away or let you leave. It would've been better for us both if I had just let you go all of those times."

I scoff at his response as my eyes begin to water. "Why would you say that? Especially right after we..."

"You don't even like to say the word, Everly. That's why."

"We fucked. There. Happy now? I'm so sorry if being with me didn't meet or exceed all of your expectations."

I try to wiggle free from underneath him even with most of my limbs still refusing to cooperate, but Hugo flattens his heavy body down, pinning me to the floor. His eyes narrow as he stares down at me. "What the hell are you talking about?"

"You basically just admitted that you regretted sleeping with me!"

"That's not what I meant, at least not in the way you think. I only regret that you'll hate me later for tonight."

"What...how...why would I hate you for tonight?" I ask as I reach up to stroke my fingers over his fuzzy jaw. "That was amazing, Hugo."

His lips twitch as he unravels my hair from his finger, then he says, "Yeah, it was, wasn't it?" easing most of the tension in me.

Tugging his beard to pull those smiling lips down, I kiss him and then ask, "Why didn't you leave town yet?"

"Because my gut told me to stay, that I'm meant to be here at least for a little longer."

"Just a little longer?"

Dropping his face to my neck, he brushes a kiss over my neck. "I think I want to stay as long as you'll let me."

"Yeah?" I ask, a grin spreading across my face when he nods his head. "In that case, I don't ever want you to leave."

Hugo lifts his face and opens his mouth, sucking in air as if he's about to say something deep and meaningful before he pushes himself off of me, sitting back on his heels. "You're really okay with everything that happened tonight?"

"I am, yeah," I tell him instead of pushing him to talk to me, to say whatever he was getting ready to say.

"Okay. Good. Now, how about we leave the floor and give the bed a try?"

"That sounds like a great idea."

There's something Hugo is not telling me, either about what happened tonight or something else entirely. I have to trust that he'll talk to me when he's ready. Until then, I just want to enjoy being with him while I can.

CHAPTER TWENTY-SIX

Everly

Rusty's death goes by with no one even raising an eyebrow in town. I didn't go to the funeral, so I don't know if it's true or not, but Taylor told me that she heard no one showed up at the memorial service other than the guy who runs the funeral home. Even the preacher was a no-show.

I can't say I'm all that surprised, especially not after the sheriff told everyone what was in the house when he and his deputies went in to see if it may have been 'a suicide.' They decided it was 'inconclusive' and dropped the case.

Anywhere else there would be a full investigation ongoing for such a strange death, but not in our small town.

Here in Rockland, we all stick together no matter what, and psychotic sex freaks are shunned even in death.

We're still trying to figure out what will happen with the house I was renting with lawyers and the bank, but they're hopeful that Harley and I won't have to move.

Although Hugo assured me that he removed all the cameras in the house, I still had to climb up the step ladder to check every air vent myself before I could sleep there again. I probably wouldn't have been able to even do that without Hugo in bed next to me.

Every night he's stayed after Harley goes to sleep. Then, when my weekday alarm goes off at six a.m., he kisses me goodbye, and then his motorcycle rumbles to life outside before he rides back to his motel room.

Unlike before when I would go days without hearing from him, Hugo sends me text messages several times a day to just check in. And I no longer have to ask him if he'll join us for dinner since he hasn't missed a single one.

The weather is starting to cool down as we get closer to the holidays. But the next Saturday is particularly nice, so Hugo, Harley and I pack up our lunch and take it down to the beach. It's too cold for Harley to swim, but she loves building sandcastles.

It's exactly the type of relaxing afternoon I think we all needed, soaking up the sun while working together. We're building the fourth castle tower when Harley tells Hugo, "There's a daddy/daughter dance at my school soon."

"Oh yeah?" Hugo replies, rubbing his hands together to clear the damp sand from them.

"Yeah. Could you go with me, even though you can't dance?" she asks, making my breath catch.

"Harley..." I start.

"What?" she questions me. "He's big and tall and looks like a daddy."

"Yes, but he's not..."

This time it's Hugo who interrupts me. "When is the dance?"

Harley looks to me, waiting for me to answer his question. "It's two weeks from today, but..."

"I'll make you a deal," Hugo tells her. "If I'm still in town the day of the dance, I'll take you."

"You will?" Harley's big brown eyes grow even wider.

"Yeah, kid, I will."

The next second Harley launches herself at him, hugging him around his neck.

I'm thankful for his offer, but for some reason it worries me, the way he prefaced it with 'if I'm still in town.' If Hugo leaves before that night, Harley will be devastated.

And so will I.

Sure, Hugo has been coming over and spending every night with us, but that could change at any moment. Then, it'll be back to the waiting and wondering, trying to explain to Harley why he's no longer around like I have to do when her own mother comes and goes unexpectedly.

While the sex with Hugo has been just as amazing as the first time, it's the naked cuddles afterward that are even better and much more dangerous.

I never knew how empty my bed could be until this morning when he kissed me goodbye and left before Harley got up since there was no alarm or rush to get ready for school.

CHAPTER TWENTY-SEVEN

Hugo

I think I want to stay in Rockland for good.

Of course, if Harley is my kid, I will definitely sell my house in Myrtle Beach and move up here. But even if I'm not the father, I don't want to leave Everly or Harley.

In fact, the past two weeks that I've been crashing in Everly's bed every night I've become more and more certain that I'm going to do it.

I'm going to call Abel and Nolan to tell them, then talk to Roman and Torin Fury about starting a new Savage Kings chapter if Remy and his brothers are interested. The five of us would be enough to get one going and that way I won't give up all of my ties to my best friends.

Now I just need to talk to Everly to see if that's something she wants. If so, once I move here, then I'll finally take the paternity test and deal with the fallout either way.

I'm planning to talk to her about it all Friday night after we read Harley's bedtime story and tuck her in, before I hear *her* voice.

It's just as loud and obnoxious as I remember as Ev and me both hurry to let her in the house so she'll stop pounding on the front door.

"I can't believe you changed the locks on me, you little bitch! Open up."

"Oh god. I'm so sorry, Hugo," Everly tells me as I let her work the locks on the door and I try to figure out if I should make a run out the back or not. "That's my lovely sister, so I have to let her in."

"Yeah, okay."

Sweat is already beading along my hairline when Everly says, "Prepare yourself for Hurricane Felicity," then pulls the door open.

"Finally!" Felicity exclaims before throwing her arms around her sister's neck so hard they both stumble backward. I'm hit with a whiff of alcohol, telling me she's not just in her normal belligerent state but also drunk. Like usual, she's dressed in the smallest pink and black dress ever made and sky-high heels that are giving her trouble. "Miss me?" she asks Ev when she shoves her away as fast as she grabbed her.

"Uh-huh. Listen, Felicity, Harley's already gone to sleep, so can you keep your voice down?"

"Already? The sun hasn't even set yet!" she remarks.

"We have a routine that we have to stick to even on weekends."

"God, you're so fucking boring, staying home on a Friday night," Felicity says with a roll of her eyes, her gaze finally landing on me. "Ooh, who is this?" she asks. "You finally landed a man? About time."

Oh, thank fuck. She's either too drunk or too stupid to remember me.

"Felicity, this is my...boyfriend?" Everly looks to me for confirmation.

"Ah, yeah, boyfriend works."

"Really? Are you sure?" Ev asks.

Before I can answer her and tell her she can call me anything she wants as long as I get to stay in her life, Felicity jumps in.

"Wait a second. You...you look familiar. Do I know you?" Felicity sidles up to me, her hips moving in that sexy way to try and draw my attention to them even though she's staggering. Unfortunately, for her, the flirty whore routine doesn't work on me anymore. Not just because Everly's so much sexier, but because she's the only woman I want, possibly ever.

My heart is about to thump out of my chest the longer Felicity stares at me from only a few inches away from my face. Here's hoping she doesn't remember how she knows me. Not yet. I just need a chance to tell Everly everything first.

Unfortunately, Felicity snaps her fingers and poof, there goes my chance. "I remember now!" She grabs my beard and tugs on it hard. "Your beard was a little shorter back then, but I bet your cock is still just as long. How's your green-eyed friend? The one who loved it up the ass?"

"Felicity!" Everly exclaims. "Watch your mouth. And, Hugo, I'm so sorry. Just ignore my sister. She's obviously very, very drunk."

"I am drunk," Felicity agrees with a giggle while slapping per palm against my chest. "Not so drunk I don't remember the Savage King *Huge-Ohhh* here making me come on his huge dick or with his big tongue. That's how I remembered his name. Get it?"

"Everly," I start, but the drunk stripper isn't finished yet.

"Don't worry, sis," she says, walking away from me to go pat her sister's shoulder. "It was a long time ago, right Huge-Oh? When even were all those crazy hot threesomes with you and the other biker? Three or four years ago? I was still living in Cape Cartwright back then I think. Everything is so blurry right now."

"You two...you really know each other?" Everly asks me, her face looking so shocked and confused that it physically hurts. I really should've been honest when it was just the two of us instead of having it come out like this.

"Ah, yeah, unfortunately," I answer with a heavy sigh.

"When?" Everly demands as she crosses her arms over her chest.

"About five years ago..." I correct Felicity, figuring there's no point in lying about it any longer.

"Five? No," Everly shakes her head as she looks between us. "No! That's...that's impossible!"

"Ev, baby, I was going to tell you, I swear!" I assure her. When I take a step toward her, Everly holds up her palm to stop me in my tracks.

"You were going to tell me that you slept with my sister? That you might be...you could be..." she trails off, unable to even say it. "When Hugo? When were you going to tell me?" she exclaims. "You've had plenty of chances while we were sleeping together these past few weeks, and you never said a word!"

"You slept with us both? No way!" Felicity chimes in with a giggle. "That's too funny!"

Ignoring her, I remind Everly, "In case you forgot, I tried to turn you down, to end this before it even started. You were persistent, and I'm glad, because being with you and Harley these past few weeks have been the best of my life!"

"What are you two talking about?" Felicity asks. "Oh, right!" She comes over and looks up at my face, then points a finger at my chest. "You might be the guy who knocked me up! Asshole. You almost ruined my life!"

"God, Felicity!" Everly shouts. "How can you say that about your daughter?"

"Oh, please. Don't even start lecturing me about my life choices."

"You still don't get it! Everything is not always about you, Felicity!" Everly says, then she turns those heated eyes toward me. "And you, you need to leave."

"Ev," I start.

She closes her eyes, and when they open again, there's nothing but loathing and anger in them. "Get out of my house!"

CHAPTER TWENTY-EIGHT

Everly

"What are you doing here Felicity?" I ask my sister while swiping my fingers underneath my eyes to wipe away my tears. I still can't believe Hugo slept with my sister and didn't tell me! He obviously came to town because he thought he might be Harley's father and didn't mention a word about it to me. God, I feel so stupid.

"I, ah, I just missed you and my little girl," my sister lies through her perfect teeth.

"Try again," I mutter.

"Jeez, sis. What's with the attitude?"

"I don't know, Felicity. Maybe I'm just so fed up with your bullshit that I can't take another second of it! All my life you've been the center of attention, the one everyone wanted to be with, the one everyone slept with. You are just so selfish, and you never take any responsibility for your actions! Well, I'm sick and tired of being your doormat. I'm not giving you a penny. And I don't want you to see Harley again."

Felicity scoffs before she flops down on the sofa, not caring that her dress is so short her panties are showing. "You can't do that to me! She's my daughter."

It's nearly impossible to keep my cool and my voice down, but I somehow manage. "No, she's mine. I'm the one who has been raising her since the day she was born. You may have given birth to her, but she's always been mine."

Glaring up at me with black mascara smeared around her brown eyes and red lipstick staining her mouth, she says, "I could take her away from you forever if I wanted."

I swallow around the knot in my throat at her threat while shaking my head. "You wouldn't dare because you don't know the first thing about being a parent, putting someone else's life before yours!"

"I could figure it out," she replies, crossing one leg over the other. "And if Hugo or that other biker is her father, then I can get child support from them. Too bad I didn't know where to find them when I was pregnant, and then he just shows up at your house four years later. Crazy huh?"

Oh god. She named her daughter after the motorcycles the possible fathers ride, not the DC character. I should've known.

"And Harley could finally have the father she's been wishing for. Isn't that what you meant?"

"Yeah, whatever."

If my blood pressure gets any higher, I'm going to freaking explode as I pace back and forth across the living room floor.

I can't let Felicity take Harley from me. If she ever got her shit together and wanted to move in with us and be a mother, I would agree to that. But if she thinks she's going to take her from me to use her as a pawn to get paid, she's got another thing coming.

That's when I realize exactly what I need to do.

I hate giving her another dime but if that's what it takes, so be it.

"I'll pay you ten thousand dollars to sign your parental rights over to me."

"Ten thousand?" Felicity repeats, her dark eyes widening in surprise. "In cash?"

"Yes, in cash."

"Deal," she says faster than I expected.

For Harley's sake, I wish Felicity wanted to be around and be a mother. But she doesn't and she never will.

"Once you sign the rights over, I want you to stay away from us."

"Fine."

"Fine," I reply in relief as I rub my fingers over my throbbing head.

Yes, it will suck to give her every penny I have in savings. But Harley and I will get by. We'll make it month-to-month as long as it takes.

For some stupid reason, my thoughts go to Hugo, and how it was so nice to have him around for a few weeks, being in Harley's life and mine.

But we're better off without that lying asshole too.

Why did he even stay for so long? He should've asked for the test and then left instead of screwing around with me, letting me make a fool of myself.

It didn't make sense why he was so hot and cold. Now it does.

And no matter how badly Harley wants a father, I can't figure out if I want Hugo to be hers or not.

Hugo

BACK AT MY MOTEL ROOM, I pack my things up and then sit down on the mattress to finally do what I've been avoiding for weeks.

195

I call Abel.

He answers after just a few rings. "Where the hell have you been?" he asks.

"Abel..." I start, but when I pause to try and figure out how to tell him this, he starts rambling.

"Man, I'm so glad to hear from you. And, ah, listen, there's something I need to tell you before you hang up..."

"There's something I have to tell you too," I reply.

"Let me go first," he says before blurting out what he's been keeping from me for years. "I'm bisexual. I know I should've told you that before today. I'm sorry I didn't, I just didn't want it to change anything between us."

"Abel..."

"I'll understand if it does change shit. I would hate it, but I would get it. I know it's weird as shit for you since we had threesomes together and all..."

"Abel, stop talking for a second!" I yell at him. "I already figured as much. Why do you think I wanted to stop the threesomes?"

"Huh?"

Dropping my head into my free hand, I tell him, "I wanted you to figure your shit out instead of keep hiding what you really wanted behind me and the threesomes! You needed to find a guy who felt the same way and could be what you needed."

"Oh. So, you knew I was attracted to men, yourself even, and that was your way of...what? Encouraging me to come out with another guy?"

"Yes. And I get that it's huge for you to finally admit to yourself and everyone else, especially the club..."

"It is. It was. But I met someone. Two people actually, Selina and, um, Cory, Rita's brother," Abel confesses, which is one hell of a surprise. Cory? The same bastard who sent Nolan to prison? I don't know how the hell that happened, but it must be one hell of a story.

"Good. Great. I'm happy for you," I say with all sincerity. "Can't wait to meet them, even the little bitch who sent Nolan to prison if you care about him, but that shit will have to wait. Right now, we've got a big fucking problem."

"Okay? What is it? Where have you been?"

"I found Felicity."

"Yeah? That's what you wanted, right?"

"She's got a daughter."

There's a moment of silence before he says, "Wow. All right. That's crazy, but it has been what? Four or five years since we saw her?"

"Do I have to fucking spell it out for you?" I snap at him, taking out my frustration with Felicity dropping by and Everly telling me to leave all on him.

"I guess you do because it sounds like you're pissed at me about something."

"Abel, *we* were with Felicity five years ago. The kid is old enough to be one of ours!"

His response is about the only one that's appropriate given the circumstances. "Oh, fuck!"

"Yeah," I agree with a heavy sigh. "I'm...I'm coming home. We can talk more when I get there," I promise him when he doesn't say anything else for several minutes.

"Seriously? You're just going to drop that little grenade on me after going missing for weeks?"

"I'm sorry. I didn't want to worry you until I knew if there was actually something to worry about. But, ah, then I talked to Felicity a little while ago, and she acted like there is a good chance it was one of us."

"That one of us could be the father of *her child*?"

"Yes, her daughter Harley. I mean, I thought the girl's name could've been a clue..."

"You fucking think!" Abel exclaims.

"But today was the first time I actually got to talk to the woman!"

"What the fuck have you been doing all this time then?"

"I, ah, I got to town and sort of started dating Felicity's sister Everly."

"You're dating the sister of the woman you may have knocked up?"

"Yes."

"Does she know?"

"Well, she does as of about ten minutes ago."

"Shit. I'm guessing she wasn't happy about that."

"No, she wasn't," I mutter.

"You like her."

"What?"

"I can hear it in your voice. You like the sister. Maybe even love her?"

"Maybe, yeah. But what the fuck does it matter now? I never got the chance to tell her the truth. I wanted to; I just wasn't sure what to say without her freaking out. Now, she'll never forgive me."

"And she's going to be a big part of your life if you're the kid's dad."

"Yep."

"So, you're really coming home now?"

"I thought we could get our paternity test together. Is that stupid? I just, I didn't want to do this alone, you know?"

"I don't want to fucking do it at all!" Abel yells through the phone. "I'm finally happy with a man and a woman. Do you know what kind of farfetched fantasy that was for me growing up? Not just being with a man but loving one enough to tell everyone and actually be with him? What am I going to do if I have a kid up in, where the fuck have you been again?"

"Rockland, Virginia. It's north of Virginia Beach, so about six hours from Myrtle..."

"Six fucking hours! If I have a kid six hours away, am I going to have to move up there?"

"I don't know what will happen, Abel. I really don't," I tell him.

"First things first, we have to go and take a test, let them send in Harley's swab and then see if one of us is a match."

"Jesus," he grumbles. "I can't believe I might have a kid. Or that you've known for what, weeks and didn't tell me?"

"I'm sorry. I swear I was just trying to keep you in the dark until I thought there was a chance..."

"You should've told me sooner," he snaps. "Did you know before you left town?"

"I saw Everly, Felicity's sister on television trying to find Harley's father. They showed a picture of Felicity and said she got knocked up five years ago."

"When?"

"When did I see the show?"

"Yes."

"Ah, the afternoon before Nolan's wedding."

"Fuck."

"I'm sorry," I tell him again. "But you can't be all that mad at me for keeping this a secret for a few weeks when you've been keeping secrets from me for years!"

"That's different and you know it!" he shouts. "Me being bisexual didn't have anything to do with you. This does affect me!"

"Fine, but if I had told you, then you wouldn't have been in town to meet and be with your new guy and girl, right?"

"Asshole," he huffs, and I know that he'll get over it, probably by the time I get back to Myrtle Beach.

"I know this is a lot to take in. Believe me, I've been trying to come to terms with it for weeks and I'm still not sure if I'm ready for the results. But Harley, she's amazing. Beautiful and tough as nails like her mama."

"You want to be her father, don't you?"

I cough out something that sounds like a laugh, but I can't even try to deny it. "If you had asked me that question a month ago, I would've said hell no. Now, though, yeah, I think I want to be her father. She's already got me wrapped around her little finger. And if I am her father, then Everly won't be able to keep her from me or avoid me. If I'm not and you are..."

"It would really complicate shit for both of us," Abel finishes for me.

"Yeah, pretty much."

"Get your ass home, man. You've been gone too long."

"See you soon," I tell him before ending the call.

What I don't say is that Myrtle Beach doesn't feel like my home anymore.

That shitty little house where Everly and Harley live has become my home. I haven't been away but for a few minutes and I already miss the hell out of them.

CHAPTER TWENTY-NINE

Everly

"A re you mad at Hugo because he lied or because he slept with your sister?" Taylor asks me. I called her and told her what happened over the weekend, how screwed up everything was, but we couldn't get together for a face-to-face therapy session until tonight after I tucked Harley into bed.

"Both!" I answer.

She gives me a head tilt. "Okay, so I get why he lied about being a potential father. Finding that out after five years would be a huge shock, I'm sure."

"Right."

"But Felicity? She's a stripper. He's a biker. I don't think it's that big of a surprise," Taylor remarks, making my mouth fall open.

"Well, I do! I thought he was a good man, one who didn't want to rush into sex with me because he cared about my feelings. That was all bullshit! He knew I would hate him if we slept together and I found out that he screwed Felicity."

"And he was obviously right," she says softly.

"Whose side are you on here?" I huff at her.

Holding up both of her palms in surrender, my best friend says, "Fine. Keep being mad at Hugo if it means not having you pissed at me."

"I'm not pissed at you," I say with a sigh. I run my fingers through my hair, pushing it out of my face. "I'm just..."

"Hurt? Angry? Sad?"

"Yes, all of the above," I agree as I slump down even further into the sofa, wishing it would swallow me whole. "Mostly I think I'm mad at myself."

"Yourself? Why?"

"Because I acted like such an idiot. Hugo kept turning me down, and I wouldn't give up."

"Oh, don't blame yourself for that," Taylor says as she comes to sit down beside me and puts her arm around my shoulders. "You liked him, and he obviously liked you too. Otherwise, he wouldn't have cared about how upset you would be when you found out."

I shake my head. "He had threesomes with her and some other biker! I was never his type. Felicity was his type."

"No, she wasn't. He doesn't care about her. He has feelings for you," Taylor remarks. When I don't bother to refute that, she goes on to ask, "What are you going to do if Hugo turns out to be Harley's father? Or if his biker friend is the father? In either of those scenarios, he'll be in your life."

A shrug is my only response.

"Come on, Everly. You can be mad at Hugo all day today and even tomorrow. But eventually you're going to have to let go of your feelings and do what's best for Harley."

"Oh god." Burying my face in my hands, I mutter, "I'm acting so selfish, just like Felicity!"

"No, you are *nothing* like your sister. You're reacting like any woman scorned would and eventually you'll figure out a way to let those feelings go for the benefit of a four-year-old girl because you love her and would do anything for her."

"I would," I agree as I lift my head, tears swimming in my eyes.

"I know you would," Taylor says with a smile. Covering my hand with hers she says, "You'll do anything for Harley because you're her mother in every way that matters."

"Even if that anything is letting a man into her life who broke my heart?"

"Exactly."

"I don't know how I'll do that. Just seeing him again is going to be hard," I tell her. "Watching him be a father to Harley for the rest of her life is going to suck for me. But at least she'll be happy. I mean, assuming that he's actually going to step up and *be* a father to her if he is her father."

"Based on what you've told me about him, I think he will. And I think he'll even move up here for good."

"No way. His priority is the MC down in South Carolina."

"Everly, he just spent weeks up here without even knowing if he's her father or not. If he is, well, he'll figure out a way to be around all of the time. That is, if you're going to let him?"

I nod and swipe away the moisture from underneath each of my eyes. "Of course I would let him be in her life as much as he wants. After five years...they've got a lot of time to catch up on."

"Yes, they do."

"And if he's not her father?" I ask my best friend.

"Then you'll get to decide what's best for you. Either you forgive him, or you forget him."

I huff out a non-humorous laugh. "I'm not sure if I could ever forget him."

"Then I guess you've got your answer," she remarks.

"No. I didn't say I could forgive him."

"Well, girl, it's got to be one of the two! Holding on to that anger isn't good for you."

"So, you think I should forgive him? Just ignore the fact that he lied to me for weeks and that he slept with my sister?"

"If you think he did those things to be cruel, to hurt you on purpose, then you should never forgive him, but you would have to eventually let him go and move on."

"I wish I could snap my fingers and forgive. I just, I can't."

"I don't blame you. I didn't say you had to forgive him this week or even this year. He lost your trust. It's up to him to work to make it up to you and restore it."

"Yeah, I just don't know if that's something Hugo would do."

"Then I guess we'll just have to wait and see," she replies. "Which reminds me, when will you get the paternity test results?"

"I sent in Harley's sample this morning. It'll take about three business days once they get their tests done." I grab my cell phone from the coffee table and pull up the text message log. "Hugo sent me a text that they were going first thing tomorrow morning."

"Good. He's still communicating with you."

"That's all he's said really."

"That's all? Just that they're going to take a test?" she asks, her brow raised in question.

"Okay, so fine! He's also sent about a dozen apologizes and called me a few times, left several messages begging me to call him back."

"I knew it! At least he feels guilty."

"Yeah, well, he *should* feel guilty."

"He's probably miserable. Did you think about that? He obviously cared about you, or he wouldn't have kept something so important from you, knowing it would make you hate him."

"I don't hate him," I admit softly.

"You could never hate anyone, not even your pain in the ass parents or sister."

"I'm not so sure about that. I'm pretty close to hate when it comes to Felicity." Biting down on my bottom lip, I debate whether or not I should tell Taylor what I did. "I, ah, found a way to get her out of Harley's life for good."

"You did? That's great, Ev. I've seen how hard it is on Harley when she shows up out of nowhere and then leaves a few days later. It confuses her."

"That's exactly what I said. Felicity needs to be part of her life consistently or not at all."

"And she chose not at all?"

"Yes," I answer. "After I agreed to give her everything in my savings account."

"Oh my god, Everly! What were you thinking?"

"I was thinking that it was what was best for Harley. A lawyer drew up some papers Monday so that I'm now her legal guardian and Felicity has no parental rights. That's worth every penny I spent."

"She should've signed the papers for nothing as much as you've done to help her!" Taylor huffs.

"Felicity would never do anything unless she got something out of it for herself."

"True and sad." Taylor gives me a smile and says, "I'm happy you have legal rights. I know that's been something that you've worried about if anything happened…"

"Worried about? It kept me up at night!" I remark as I get to my feet and pace, recalling those horrible what if scenarios. "My worst nightmare was Felicity finding Harley's biological father and taking her away from me to get child support."

"That's what she was going to do if Hugo or his friend were the father, wasn't she?"

"Yes."

"God, she is such a b-i-t-c-h."

"Don't I know it," I agree.

205

CHAPTER THIRTY

Hugo

"So now we wait?" Abel asks when we leave the testing facility and step out into the cool morning sun.

"Yeah. We just have to wait three business days for the results."

"And have you decided what you'll do if you're her father?"

"Not yet," I answer.

"You must have thought about it on the ride home, right?"

"I guess I would want to live in Rockland with them. With Harley," I amend but not fast enough based on Abel's knowing grin.

"You love her. The sister. You want to move up there to be a happy little family."

I shrug and glance away toward our bikes. "That wouldn't be as bad as I once thought it would be."

"What about the Savage Kings?"

"You think I haven't thought about them too?" I reply. "I don't know what I would do about the Kings. I mean, the closest chapter is

Norfolk, which isn't a long ride. I could go nomad again or see about starting a new chapter..."

"Just like that you would up and leave me?" Abel asks.

"If she's my daughter, then yeah I would."

"And if she's mine?" he asks.

"Then fuck if I know."

"I'm sorry shit is so complicated for you," Abel remarks. "If I could snap my fingers and make you the daddy, you know I would."

"Yeah, I know. You've got a good thing here with Selina opening up the bed and breakfast and visiting Cory in Georgia until he graduates. If you're her father, then everything would be up in the air."

"Yeah, it would suck, but we would figure it out. That's how much I love them both, you know? They were both there when you called, and I found out I might be her father. The first thing Cory said was that it would take more than a kid to scare him away," Abel tells me with a grin. "And Selina, well, she's ready to be a stepmother, no doubt about it."

"I'm glad you have two people who love you," I tell him honestly. "One would've never been enough."

"Yeah, I think you're right about that. I would've always been missing something either way I went..."

"So, you get the best of both worlds. You're lucky."

Slapping a hand on my shoulder, he says, "This girl, Everly, if it's the real thing, she'll forgive you."

"You think so?" I ask him.

"Hell, I know it for a fact."

"I really hope you're right."

~

Hugo

I've been staring at my phone all day, waiting.

It's been three business days since Abel and I had our paternity tests done at the lab. The wait has nearly killed me. Today, I haven't even been able to function or do anything but sit on the sofa, constantly refreshing my email over and over again while court shows and *Meloney* play in the background.

"Anything yet?" Abel asks as he comes through the front door without knocking. Why would he? He still has a key and used to live here even if it were locked.

"No. Nothing yet," I tell him.

"I take it you haven't had anything to eat or showered today?" he says as he takes a seat in the chair.

I look up from the phone screen, surprised to see he's alone, and shake my head, trying to recall the last meal I had.

"I think I ate an ice cream sandwich yesterday."

"Jesus, man!" Abel exclaims. "You need to eat something before you pass out. Want me to make something?"

"No thanks. I think I might throw up if I eat even a bite of food." I refresh my email and there's nothing new, so I look up to ask, "Aren't you nervous?"

"Hell yes! But Cory and Selina have kept me busy the last three days. We stayed with Cory at school so I wouldn't be pulling my hair out here. He wanted to help but couldn't miss any classes..." Abel stops talking and winces. "Do you mind me talking about him? Is it weird?"

"You love him. He's part of your life. It's not weird for you to talk about him."

"Are you sure?"

"I don't care, man. You know that. I mean, I do care, about you. As long as you're happy, then it doesn't matter if you have a hundred lovers, and more than half are men."

Abel barks out a chuckle. "Not a hundred. Just two. I don't need anyone else to make me happy."

"I'm surprised they didn't come with you over here."

"Selina wanted to. Cory even offered to miss classes today, but I told them both we should do this alone, just the two of us."

"Yeah, I get that," I say just as my phone dings loudly, nearly making my heart leap out of my chest.

Abel and I stare wide-eyed at each other for a silent second. "It's probably just junk mail," I tell him as I make my eyes lower to the screen again. I see the word "lab" in the sender's name and start breathing so fast I go lightheaded. "It's the results."

"Well? Open them already. The suspense is killing me!" Abel says. "Do you want me to do it?"

"No, no. I'll do it. Just, give me a second," I reply as close my eyes and take a few deep, slow breaths to keep from hyperventilating. Then, I look down at the phone and click to open the email.

There's a bunch of numbers and shit I don't understand. Then I get to the last line which says, *"The probability of paternity is zero percent."*

Fuck.

"Hugo?" Abel asks. "What does it say?"

Before I can answer him, his own phone dings from his cut pocket.

He fumbles with the device as he tries to hurry up and get it out. With a few taps, his eyes are bulging, his lips are mouthing the words silently. He stops and says, "The probability of paternity is 99 percent with bunch of nines after the decimal. Does that mean..."

He looks up at me and I nod.

I have to clear my throat to tell him, "You're Harley's father," because it feels like everything I've ever wanted is slipping through my fingers like sand.

"Jesus Christ!" Abel shouts as he drops the phone on his lap and leans back, both palms scrubbing over his face.

"I'm sorry."

"I can't believe it. I can't fucking believe it," he mumbles before finally dropping his hands to look at me. "It should be you! You want to be her father, and I hardly ever fucked Felicity in any way that makes a kid!"

"Yeah, I know," I reply quietly.

"I'm so sorry, Hugo. If I could trade places with you, I would do it in a heartbeat. You know that, right?"

"Yeah, I know."

"Just as everything was starting to be going great here now, I'm going to have to...I may need to move to Virginia! And Selina is about to get the bed and breakfast up and going. Cory still has months of college. We'll be so far away, visiting won't be as easy," he rambles before finally shaking his head. "Shit. I'm sure Selina and Cory will be okay with whatever I have to do for the kid, you know? And will the sister want me to pay child support?"

"I-I don't know."

"Fuck, Hugo. Are you going to be okay?"

"Hmm, let's see, the woman I love hates my guts, and the only possible way I could get back into her life was to be the father of her sister's child. But I'm not, so, that's that. I don't know what the fuck to do now."

"You'll figure it out."

"I had it figured out!" I shout at him, knowing it's wrong to take my anger out on him when it's not his fault his sperm somehow made it to Felicity's pussy but mine didn't. "Everly's cousins all ride Harleys. There's, like, four of them and then their friends, enough to make a new Savage Kings chapter up in Rockland."

"You were really going to start a new chapter up there?" Abel asks.

"Yeah, I thought about it. I was going to talk to Roman if I was Harley's father, see if Torin and the Emerald Isle originals would approve it. Now...it doesn't fucking matter."

"It could still matter," Abel says. "We could both move up there and start the new club together."

"You've never even been there. How do you know if you'll want to live there for good?" I ask him. "And like you said, Cory and Selina might not want to move."

"Yeah, you're right. That doesn't mean you can't go through with your plan."

I glare at him, hoping that one day soon the jealousy I feel when I look at my best friend will lessen. "I'm not her father!"

"So fucking what?" Abel grumbles. "You wanted to be her father, right?"

"Yes."

"And I didn't. I wanted a family with Selina and Cory some day in the future. Not right now."

"Are you saying you're not going to step up to the plate?" I ask, growing even angrier, if that's fucking possible.

"No, I'm not saying that," he says as he rubs his palm over the top of his head. "Shit, man, why can't we both be her father?"

"You know I don't like dick and I'm sorry, but I never will."

Abel scoffs and rolls his green eyes. "That's not what I meant."

"Then what did you mean?" I cross my arms over my chest and wait.

"I meant, you could be her fulltime father, move up north, live nearby, see her every day, drop her off at school and pick her up."

"But I'm not..."

He holds up his palm to stop me. "I know that. And I also know that I could do it, I could pull up the roots I was starting to put down and plant them there, with or without Selina and Cory at first, and try to fill the role. But my heart wouldn't be in it. I've never even seen the girl and she's my daughter! I have a daughter! I need some time to let this sink in, to meet her, let her get to know me before I even think about picking up my life that's finally good and moving. What if she doesn't even like me?"

"I worried about the same thing, but Harley warmed right up to me. She'll love you too."

"Yeah, but what if I can't ever love her the way you already do?"

"You will."

"Hugo, man, you want this. Do me this solid, fill my shoes until I can figure this shit out. Be her father in name even if you're not by blood."

I'm already shaking my head. "Everly won't let me...she's too pissed at me."

"Then beg her to forgive your ass until she finally does it."

"I could move up there, start a chapter, do everything you just said, and it might not matter to her."

"If you don't at least give it a try, then you'll never know if you could make it work with Everly or not."

Fuck, I think he might be right.

"Fine. I'll leave tomorrow morning. There's this thing Saturday that I don't want to miss..."

"Can I come with you?" Abel asks. "To meet her?"

"You can try. It'll be up to Everly, though."

"I know," he agrees. "Let's give it a try."

CHAPTER THIRTY-ONE

Everly

"Harley, please come out so we can start getting you ready for the dance!" I call through her bedroom door.

I should've had Hugo remove the lock when he was working on the other ones.

God, when will I stop doing that – stop thinking about him all the damn time? It's been over a week since I kicked him out. He's been calling, but I still can't talk to him. I have been listening to his voicemails only to hear if he's received the paternity results yet. Thanks to the HIPAA laws, Hugo had the option to get them by email while I have to wait for them to arrive by snail mail.

"Harley?"

There's no answer, and when the doorbell rings, I have to stop coaxing her to go answer it.

As soon as I pull the door open, I'm smiling at the man on the other side because I've only ever seen him in t-shirts and jeans my entire life. Tonight, he's wearing black dress pants, a silver button down and even a tie.

"You clean up nice," I tell Remy.

"Yeah?" he asks with a grin as he straightens the tie. "I even have a jacket in the truck."

"Nice! Come on in," I tell him. "I was just trying to convince Harley to come out so we could start getting her ready. Maybe you being here will encourage her."

"I'll try my best," he says before he starts walking toward the hall to her room. Gently rapping his knuckles on the door, he says, "Hey, munchkin. Are you really going to stand me up tonight? I'm excited about going with you and have even been working on my dance moves. You want to see them?"

"*No!*" Harley's scream from the other side of the door is so loud and sudden Remy and I both jump back. "You're only a cousin, not a daddy!"

"What does that matter, Harley?" I call out. "You were going to go with Hugo, so what's the difference in going with Remy? You won't believe how fancy he looks in his tie."

"It's different!" she shouts. "None of the kids in my class know Hugo. I could tell them he's my daddy, and they wouldn't know it's a lie!"

I wince because she's breaking my heart. "It's-it's not good to lie to your friends."

A wordless, high-pitched scream is her response to that comment.

Remy mouths the word *sorry* before he wraps me up in his arms.

"Thank you for trying," I tell him softly. "I don't think she's going to come out, though."

"I know. I wish she would let me take her."

I nod, and he lets me go so that we can both head back into the living room where I sit heavily on the sofa to bury my face in my hands.

216

"She's been acting this way ever since Hugo left," I tell him. "I don't know what else to do. I took away her TV time, her car, her Harley, everything but books." I lift my head to look up at Remy, who is still standing in the middle of the room like he's trying to figure out what to do. "Do you know what she did when all she had were books?"

"What?" he asks.

"She tore out all of the pages out. Every single one."

"Jesus," Remy mutters while stroking a hand over his jaw.

"It was awful. What if...what if she gets worse? The violent outbursts, hitting kids at school, cutting them with scissors..."

"Harley is only four. She doesn't know what she's doing. The girl is just dealing with strong emotions the only way she knows how."

"She did feel bad after the book massacre."

"Yeah?"

"She got the tape out and tried to put all the pages back. Now the books are all mixed up together, with pages from ten different books in one."

"It'll be a fun new way to read them since no one will know what happens next," Remy remarks, making me laugh sadly before I hear a familiar sound from outside paralyzes me.

"What?" Remy asks, having noticed the concern on my face.

"Were you expecting your brothers to come over here?"

"No. Why?"

Since I can't seem to move, I'm glad when he goes over and looks out the window for me as the rumbly sound grows louder before shutting off completely.

"Who is it?" I ask. "Colt? Barrett? RJ?"

"Nope," Remy answers with a heavy sigh. Frowning, he looks back at me and says, "Do you want me to get rid of them?"

"Them?"

"Yeah, it's Hugo and another guy in a Savage Kings cut."

"He's really back? For the dance?"

I finally have enough strength to get to my feet and join Remy at the window. Sure enough, out in the driveway are two Harleys, two bikers, who remove their helmets and start walking toward the porch steps.

"What do you want me to do here, Ev?"

"I-I don't know? What should I do?" I ask him just as the doorbell rings.

Remy chuckles. "Hell if I know. It's up to you. I could always try and kick his ass."

I flip back and forth in my head with indecision before finally going over and jerking the door open. The men both take a few steps back, so I can come out on the porch.

My heart aches at the sight of Hugo but a part of me is happy to see him, which is so confusing that I want to scream.

"What are you doing here?" I ask, feeling Remy at my back.

"Ev," Hugo starts, his deep voice grumbly. He clears his throat and says, "Everly, I want you to meet my best friend, Abel Giovanni."

Okay... that was the last thing I expected him to say. He came back because he wants me to meet his friend?

"Hey, it's nice to finally meet you," Abel says as he extends his hand to me. When he offers me a nervous smile, I cave and shake his hand because he hasn't ever lied to me.

"Abel is Harley's father," Hugo announces quietly, the words so out of the blue I'm not sure I heard him right.

"What? He's her father?"

"Yes."

"Wh...are you sure?" I ask in disbelief. It can't be that easy, not after years and years of wondering, testing, the freaking nationwide television show...

Abel pulls out a piece of paper from inside his leather cut and hands it to me. With a shaking hand, I open it and try to make sense of the numbers and words but can't really see them. It's all just blurring together thanks to the tears welling up in my eyes, so I'll have to take their word for it.

"It's true, Ev. I wouldn't lie to you about something like this," Hugo says softly.

"Oh my god," I mutter as I look at the other man again, searching his face for similarities. Maybe it's all in my head, or it's the shadows, but I do see some of Harley in the shape of his eyes and his lips, his dark hair.

"I know you have a lot going on right now, but, um, if it's okay with you, I would really like to finally meet my daughter," Abel says, his voice hitching at the end.

"Yes, of course. Come in."

It finally occurs to me that Hugo's timing was intentional. He remembered that the dance was tonight and wanted Harley to go with her real father.

Still, I haven't had time to figure out how I feel about him yet, so I just lead them to Harley's bedroom door.

"Will you?" I ask Hugo. "She won't believe me. And Remy and I couldn't get her to come out."

"Okay, yeah," he agrees, swallowing visibly before he knocks hard on the door. "Harley, it's Hugo. Will you open up, so I can talk to..."

The door whips opens before I even hear the lock disengage.

Hugo

"You came back!" Harley says as she looks up at me with Cutie Pie the cat clutched underneath her arm.

"I did, and I brought someone with me," I tell her. I step aside so she can see Abel better.

"Ah, hey," he says with a wave of his hand.

"This is my friend, Abel. And even though it'll be hard for you to believe – he's your daddy. He took a test and all, so he could prove it to you."

"He did?" she asks, looking from me to Abel.

"Yep."

"It's true, sweetie," Everly adds. "Abel is your father."

For several long seconds Harley looks at me and then Abel silently before she throws her arms around my legs and squeezes them tight. I glance over my shoulder at Ev in confusion as I reach down to pat her back.

I thought it would be Abel she ran to and hugged, not me.

"Thank you for finding my daddy," Harley says when she throws her head back to look up at me with the biggest fucking smile I've ever seen on her face. It makes my throat and eyes burn like hell.

"Ah, well, I didn't..." I start to say, but Ev clears her throat in warning for me to just go along with it. "You...you're welcome."

When Harley lets go of my legs, she holds out her little hand to Abel. "I'm Harley. It's nice to finally meet you," she tells him.

"Yeah?" he says with a watery chuckle as he clasps her hand, swallowing it whole. "It's nice to meet you too. And that's a really cool name. Harley is also the same name of one of my most favorite things in the world."

"Really?" she asks him.

"Really."

"Harley, Abel and I were hoping we could take you to the dance tonight," I tell her. "If you still want to go and if Everly says it's okay."

"Both of you?" Harley questions with her dark eyes narrowed way too skeptically for someone so young.

"Would that be okay with you?" Everly asks. "Because it's okay with me..."

And man, that's a huge fucking relief to hear.

"Two daddies are so much better than one!" Harley exclaims excitedly as she starts twirling and jumping up and down with her arms raised in the air.

"Is now a good time to mention the future possibility of a third daddy?" Abel whispers just loud enough for me and Everly to hear him. Turning to her, he says, "You should probably know that I have a serious boyfriend, and a girlfriend in case that's a problem."

"Oh," Everly mutters. "Well, that's nice and all for you, but how about we ease her into two daddies first?"

Abel laughs and agrees while I'm still wondering if she really means that we can both be part of Harley's life. Does that mean I get to be part of Everly's too?

"Hugo, can we go talk while Abel and Harley have a moment to get to know each other?" she asks.

"Ah, sure," I agree.

Remy is still standing in the living room when we return to it.

"Glad you're back, even if my brothers and I owe you an ass-whopping," he says. "Stop by the garage when you get a minute?"

"Yeah, I will," I agree. "There's something I wanted to talk to you and your brothers about after the ass-whopping is finished."

"Oh yeah?"

"How would you feel about wearing the bearded skull king?"

Remy's eyes widen. "Patch into the Savage Kings? The nearest chapter is in Norfolk..."

"Unless we have five men here to start a new chapter," I remark.

"No shit?" he asks with a grin.

"No shit."

"I'll talk to the guys and see what they think, but I'm pretty sure it'll be a hell yes."

"Good. Being a nomad is a shitty way to live. If I get to stay here..." I trail off.

"I'll take off so you two can talk," Remy says as he glances between me and Ev. "Call me if you need me?"

"Absolutely," Ev agrees as she gives her cousin a big hug.

After he's out the door, I say, "He tried to take Harley to the dance?"

"Yes, and she turned him down," Everly replies. "Want to go out to the back porch?"

"Okay, sure," I agree as I follow her.

On the way out, I try to figure out where the hell to begin. I know I need to apologize first and foremost, even though that hasn't gotten a response from her on the phone yet.

As soon as the backdoor shuts behind me, I don't even get a single word out of my mouth before Everly grabs the back of my neck to pull my mouth down to hers. I go happily, surprised as hell that she wants to kiss me.

My hands rest gently on her hers because I'm afraid that if I touch her too much or the wrong way, she'll pull away and realize I don't deserve any more of her kisses.

But then the kiss keeps going and going, getting hotter when she adds her tongue into the mix.

I finally give up the crazy concerns I had and reach for her ass to heft her body up against mine, needing her closer.

She comes willingly, wrapping her legs around my waist and her arms around my neck. I swallow her moan that loosens the last of the tension in my body.

By the way she's clinging to me, I'm starting to think we might be good.

When we both have to finally break apart for air, Everly rests her forehead against mine and says, "Don't ever lie to me again," through her pants. "Or sleep with my sister."

"Never. I swear," I promise her, crushing her even tighter to my chest. When she buries her face against my neck and her lips kiss my skin there, I tell her. "I love you, only you. Well, only you and Harley."

She lifts her head, looking me in the eye when she says something to me no one has ever said to me before. "I love you, too."

I kiss her again, unable to believe she's willing to forgive me so easily. I don't deserve it, but I'll make sure she never regrets this particular decision.

"Abel can't move up here right away, but I can. I'll fill his shoes until he works things out, if you'll let me."

"Of course," Everly replies, her fingers pulling at my hair to bring my mouth back to hers. "Now shut up and kiss me again. Please," she whispers against my lips.

"God, yes," I agree.

CHAPTER THIRTY-TWO

Hugo

"Are you still having fun?" I ask Harley over the kiddy voices on the stereo singing a horrid rendition of "Mamacita" by the Black Eyed Peas.

"Yes!" she exclaims without pausing in her jumping, spinning dance moves that makes her red and black dress swirl around her legs. Giggling, she adds, "You and Abel dance funny!"

Unsure how we were supposed to dance, the two of us just started showing her old school moves like the Running Man, the Carlton, and the Cabbage Patch.

And honestly, I don't know how the girl has any energy left after an entire hour of making Abel and I keep up with her in the middle of the gym's dance floor. Before the dancing, Harley had a pink heart painted on her face, ate only the cheese from her slice of pizza and mine, then crammed two whole cupcakes down her throat.

We seem to be holding up better than some of the other fathers, who are guzzling punch with sweat stains under the arms of their dress shirts, but just barely.

Some of them gave us funny looks when we walked into the dance with Harley loudly announcing to the principal selling tickets at the door, along with the rest of the world, that she needed tickets for her two daddies.

I honestly don't care if they think Abel and I are a couple or not. It's a complicated situation and none of their business.

"Okay, dads! Grab your daughters for one last dance!" the principle announces over the speaker system.

"Thank goodness," Abel says. "My legs are almost numb."

I know what he means. It's been a long day, one where we spent five hours of riding our bikes up here. But I wouldn't have missed it for anything.

A slow song comes on, and as we've done for the previous ones, Harley insists on Abel and I both staying on the dance floor with her. She takes my hand and then one of Abel's to sway dramatically back and forth between us, making us both grin.

"Hold hands to make a circle!" Harley demands, so we, of course, comply.

"She's a bossy little thing, isn't she?" Abel leans over to whisper to me once our palms are clasped.

"Yeah, only because she knows we won't refuse her."

"This whole day turned out better than I expected," he says.

"Yeah, it did, didn't it?" I agree.

Harley's head leans against my arm for several long moments, then her hand in mine drops heavily.

"She's asleep standing up," Abel remarks with a chuckle.

Leaning down, I notice her eyes are closed. "I think you're right. Ready to get her home?"

"Yeah."

I start to reach down to pick her up before second-guessing the decision. "Do you want to take her to the car?"

"No, you can carry her," Abel says. "She barely knows me."

"Okay," I agree as I scoop her up in my arms and hold her against my chest.

As we start toward the exit, the principal, who is waiting next to the door, hurries to open it for me before Abel can reach it.

"Did you three have a good night?" she asks.

"We really did," I answer.

"Yeah, I'm glad I got to be here for Harley," Abel says.

"Me too," I agree as we walk out to the parking lot, heading toward Ev's car that she let us borrow tonight.

Once Harley is tucked into the backseat, I shut the door and Abel asks, "Do you think I could have dual membership, you know, a leather cut with patches for Myrtle Beach and one for up here if you start a chapter?"

"You can't be happy unless you have the best of both worlds, can you?" I tease him with a chuckle.

I'm honestly surprised by how fast Abel's brought up the topic of moving here.

But then again, that's just how persuasive our girl can be.

EPILOGUE

Hugo

To celebrate the induction of a new Savage Kings chapter, we're having a family bonfire at the beach in Rockland.

The original Kings agreed to a no prospecting period for the Fulton brothers since they considered them a previous MC, even if they were just a family who rode together. Each of us will pick a prospect soon, and a year from now, hopefully we'll have ten or more members.

Over the past few weeks, I've learned I can trust Remy and his brothers with my secrets and even my life. Killing a man together is a bonding experience. So, having me vouch for the four of them was all it took to officially start the Savage Kings MC, Rockland, Virginia chapter.

I miss Nolan and the other Myrtle Beach guys, but I'll still get to see them a few times a year.

And Abel, well, he recently introduced Cory and Selina to Harley. They're playing with her and some blown up beach balls now, ones that the ocean breeze keeps stealing away. It's already obvious that they love her as much as Abel and I do.

"How has Harley been doing in school and at home? Any, ah, behavioral issues lately?" Abel asks quietly while we watch the three of them chase the balls around.

"No issues. She's been an angel," I assure him. "Ev and I told her Felicity had to take a job faraway in the desert where there are no planes, trains, or automobiles to try and explain why she won't be coming around. We also explained that Felicity wanted Everly to be a mother to her from now on, so she has two mommies and two daddies." I smile at the memory of how maturely she handled the news, much better than we ever expected. "All Harley wanted to know after that conversation was if she could call Everly mommy now instead of Evie which, of course, made Ev ecstatic."

"Good, that's good," Abel says. "I was worried...I didn't know if she would be okay with me coming and going all of the time like Felicity."

My best friend has been visiting every other weekend for now. I step in for him every other day when he's gone.

"You are nothing like Felicity," I assure him. "You always visit when you say you will, which is exactly what Harley needs, someone who keeps their word and doesn't let her down."

"We've started looking for a house up here."

"Yeah?" I say in surprise.

"Yeah, preferably a big one with several bedrooms that only need a little work. Selina's talked me into opening up a B&B in town. We'll hire on a local to run it while we're in Myrtle but will always have a place to stay when we come visit for a few weeks. Maybe months in the summer after Cory graduates."

"That's great, man. I hope you three find something soon."

"Fuck, I do too," he says with a chuckle. "I don't know how you've stuck it out in that shitty motel for so long."

"Easy – I'm sticking it out because I love them," I explain to him. "The crappy motel is a small price to pay until I earn Everly's trust back. I'm just happy she let me back in her and Harley's life."

"Speaking of the saint," Abel remarks as Everly comes over and hands both of us cold bottles of beer. "Thanks, Ev. Looks like I'm needed to even out the teams for a game of volleyball. The girls are whopping Cory's ass."

"Have fun," Everly tells him as he walks off, saluting her with his beer bottle.

I take a sip of mine and say, "Thanks, blondie. What would I do without you?"

"Oh, I don't know," Ev replies with a grin. "Be sad and lonely? Guess that's another reason why I should give you this." She reaches into her jean pocket and then slips whatever she pulled out into the front of my jeans.

"What was that?" I ask her before shoving my fingers down in the pocket and finding...

"A key," Everly says.

"A key to visit whenever I want or..." I trail off when I pull out the gold metal and hold it up in front of my face. I already have an identical one, but that one is a key I kept when I installed the locks, not one I earned.

"No, not to visit. This is my way of asking you to move in with us. Christmas is almost here. It would be nice to be a real family for Harley for once, don't you think? Hopefully Abel, Selina and Cory can join us for a few days too."

"Are you sure you're ready for this, letting me move in?" I ask, putting the key back in my pocket to brush a long strand of her blonde hair behind her ear. "It's not too fast for you or Harley?"

"Are you planning to stay?"

"Hell yes." I turn around and show her the newly sewn on bottom rocker on my leather cut before facing her again.

"Savage Kings...Virginia? So, it's done, you started a new MC chapter?"

"It's all a done deal, baby," I tell her as I slip my arm around her waist to pull her closer to me. "That's what this bonfire with your cousins is all about. All of us are getting a chance to start a new chapter, and we're going to do it together."

The End

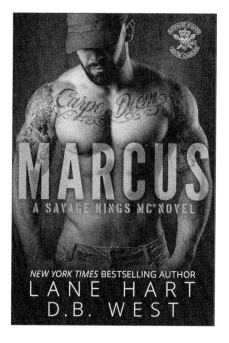

When Marcus De La Cruz volunteered to sponsor the next prospect for the Savage Kings MC, he never expected to have a female candidate. Instead of being intimidated by him, she gives as good as she gets.

Teagan Allen knows the dangers of being a member of an outlaw MC all too well since her father was killed while wearing the bearded skull king patch. Roy Allen wasn't just a member, but the president of the Charlotte chapter, and the man loved the club more than anything – even his own daughter.

Hoping to better understand her father's obsession with the biker club, Teagan is determined to wear the same coveted patch, no matter what it takes, even if she has to manipulate the man in charge of picking the new prospect.

Marcus may think he has the upper hand when it comes to his secret exploits with Teagan, but she's about to show him that more than one person can wear the crown in their relationship.

Order your copy now!

ABOUT THE AUTHORS

New York Times bestselling author Lane Hart and husband D.B. West were both born and raised in North Carolina. They still live in the south with their two daughters and enjoy spending the summers on the beach and watching football in the fall.

Connect with D.B.:
Twitter: https://twitter.com/AuthorDBWest
Facebook: https://www.facebook.com/authordbwest/
Website: http://www.dbwestbooks.com
Email: dbwestauthor@outlook.com

Connect with Lane:
Twitter: https://twitter.com/WritingfromHart
Facebook: http://www.facebook.com/lanehartbooks
Instagram: https://www.instagram.com/authorlanehart/
Website: http://www.lanehartbooks.com
Email: lane.hart@hotmail.com

Join Lane's Facebook group to read books before they're released, help choose covers, character names, and titles of books! https://www.facebook.com/groups/bookboyfriendswanted/

Find all of Lane's books on her Amazon author page!

Sign up for Lane and DB's newsletter to get updates on new releases and freebies!

Printed in Great Britain
by Amazon

68910953R00139